THE
ROOT OF
MAGIC

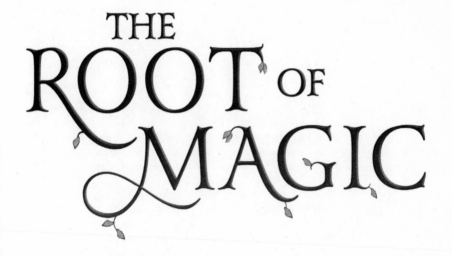

THE ROOT OF MAGIC

KATHLEEN BENNER DUBLE

Delacorte Press

Text copyright © 2019 by Kathleen Benner Duble
Jacket art copyright © 2019 by Pascal Campion

All rights reserved. Published in the United States by Delacorte Press, an imprint of Random House Children's Books, a division of Penguin Random House LLC, New York.

Delacorte Press is a registered trademark and the colophon is a trademark of Penguin Random House LLC.

rhcbooks.com

Educators and librarians, for a variety of teaching tools, visit us at RHTeachersLibrarians.com

Library of Congress Cataloging-in-Publication Data is available upon request.
ISBN 978-0-525-57850-5 (trade) — ISBN 978-0-525-57851-2 (lib. bdg.) — ISBN 978-0-525-57853-6 (ebook)

The text of this book is set in 12-point Adobe Garamond Pro.
Interior design by Jaclyn Whalen

Printed in the United States of America
10 9 8 7 6 5 4 3 2 1
First Edition

For the wondrous women of Currier's Ten Man:
Kate Beers, Ali Clarke, AJ Motgi, Delia Pais, Maren
Shapiro, Annie Shoemaker, Meg Starr, Maggie
Wollner, and Tess Wood—I want to thank you for
all the warm sunshine and laughter you have always
added to my life! And to my daughter, the tenth
woman of the ten man, Tobey Duble, who keeps this
tree of roommates firmly flowering and has always
embodied the idea that the true root of all magic is
kindness, compassion, family, and friends. I am in
awe of you all!

We must believe in free will. We have no choice.
—ISAAC BASHEVIS SINGER

CHAPTER 1

"Are we going to die?" Wisp asks from the depths of his blankets in the backseat.

Mom's hands whiten on the wheel of the car, and her mouth tightens.

In the front seat beside their mother, Willow tugs nervously on her long hair.

DuChard *Unspoken* Family Rule #1: You are never, ever to say the words "death" or "die" when Wisp is within earshot.

But because Wisp himself is asking the question, Mom has no option but to pretend she hasn't heard him.

"Of course not," Willow tells her brother, when their mom says nothing. "It's just snow, Wisp."

Yet even as she tries to convince her brother, Willow realizes she is lying. They have been driving in the dark for over two hours in what the weathermen on the radio are calling "the blizzard of the century."

It is four days after Christmas, and the first storm of the year. Usually, a December snowfall in the Northeast tumbles in like a light blanket, one you pull up just as the temperature begins to dip—fluffy but not too heavy.

But this storm is monstrous. Willow imagines it as a great roaring beast—irritated by the release of aerosols in Russia, the exhaust of cars in China, the heat of nuclear reactors in the United States, and other global warming factors.

Her science teacher has said that hurricanes, fires, and tsunamis have been increasing in number and intensity. Why, Willow wonders, should snow sit on the sidelines?

When they left that afternoon, the flakes were light. Then the weather changed—faster than they could change their plans. Now Willow wishes they had stayed the night in some safe, warm hotel in Canada. But it's too late. They are committed to driving home.

Usually on car trips, Willow listens to music or writes in her journal, but tonight she simply stares into the dark night and icy roads, preparing to point out any danger that might suddenly throw them off course.

"Do you think we're going to be swallowed up by this storm and suffocate in this car?" her brother asks. His weary voice floats softly up to the front seat. "Are they going to find us months from now, when everything melts, just skeletons, since we have no food and only a few bottles of water?"

In the front seat, Willow rolls her eyes at her brother's bizarre questions.

"Don't be silly, Wisp," their mom finally snaps.

But a minute later, she sighs and rubs her eyes. "Sorry, I didn't mean to yell. I'm just tense from driving."

Willow says nothing. She knows she is to blame for their being on this road at this hour, just below the Canadian border in the wilderness of Maine, where even their car's headlights seem unable to penetrate the wall of white in front of them.

"Dad can drive in anything," Wisp says.

Willow goes still.

DuChard *Unspoken* Family Rule #2: Never mention Dad in front of Mom, especially when she is already under so much stress that the lines on her face look like cracked dry clay.

"Do you *see* your father here?" Mom asks.

Her brother goes mute, seeming to recognize his mistake, leaving Willow to answer her mom.

Willow should call out her brother for this cowardliness, but she won't. Instead, as usual these days, she swallows her annoyance with him, forcing the heat of it back inside.

She shakes her head as a response. It's safer that way. And she realizes in that moment that she, like her brother, is a bit of a coward these days, too.

"It was your *father's* last-minute cancellation that left us having to drive all the way to New Brunswick for this hockey tournament in the first place," their mother goes on, in the tone that Willow has come to know as worse than the taste of sour milk. "He *could* have made that decision earlier, and then you *could* have ridden with one of your teammates. But no, once again, he waits until the last minute. And now, as usual, he's nowhere to be found, leaving me on my own, driving through a horrific storm while he's holed up in some basketball court, all warm and toasty. And it was his idea that you play hockey in the first place, so I really don't understand why it's me doing the hauling around, especially with a . . ."

Their mother goes suddenly silent.

In her mind, Willow finishes the sentence for her mother. ". . . with a sick child."

"Whatever," Mom finally says softly. "Your dad should be here, not me."

DuChard *Unspoken* Family Rule #3: When their mom starts going on about their dad, it's best to act like you're facing an angry bear and, as Willow's Girl Scout leader once told them, "Hold perfectly still and play dead."

So Willow turns statuelike, and she thinks about the game. The game they won—the big save she made.

Willow can still feel the puck hitting hard against her glove as she raised it a few inches above her shoulder. And she remembers the complete and utter amazement when she realized the puck was there—safe, stopped, just as the buzzer sounded and the game ended. Incredibly, they had won by that one, single stopping of a goal.

Willow can still hear the crowd screaming her name and feel her best friend, Elise, jumping on top of her before the rest of the team piled on, all smelling of sweat from their hard-won battle. It had been a sweet save, a sweet win.

4

And Willow wishes her dad *had* been there. Because, unlike her mom, he would have known that feeling, understood that victory, cheered her on as a winner. He'd played hockey in college. He knew.

But he couldn't find a substitute to coach his high school basketball team this weekend. Instead, it was her mom waiting for her at the end of the game, tapping her foot during the winning-team pictures, shooing Willow off the ice, urging her to change quickly, barely able to wait half an hour before packing them up and starting the drive home, worrying and fussing about the snow.

Now, with this scary drive, the joy of that miracle win in Willow's otherwise miracleless life has deflated quickly, like bubble gum that has gone flat and tasteless.

"Are we going to be lost forever?" Wisp asks.

He must feel that even though the blizzard is still raging outside their car, the "Mom storm" has passed, but Willow isn't so sure.

"Maybe we'll be like Rip Van Winkle and get lost in these hills and sleep for centuries," Wisp says.

"Rip Van Winkle left his poor wife alone to handle everything herself while he was out having a good time and a long nap," Mom snaps again.

As Willow thought: her brother was wrong. Neither storm is backing off.

"I would like to nap like that," he whispers.

This shuts their mother up. Willow glances back at her

5

brother, his little body curled tight on the seat, and he gives her a weak smile. Dark circles ring his eyes—constant reminders of his sickness. No doctor has been able to pinpoint what is wrong with him, even though they've done plenty of tests.

Once, Willow overheard a doctor tell Wisp he had a "rare disease" because he was a rare kid. She knows the doctor only said that to make Wisp feel special. But sometimes she remembers that comment to make herself feel better too, especially when her brother looks really pale—kind of like he does now.

Willow glances over to where their mom sits, tense and worried, both hands on the wheel. The coffee she bought earlier at a rest stop grows cold in its cup holder; her eyes are focused on the road as if her will alone can guarantee their safety. Her mom—the battler of battles, the gladiator in all their lives.

If Mother Nature bothered to show herself now in the midst of this storm and challenged Willow's mom to hand-to-hand combat, her mom would quickly tie these dark clouds into tight knots, blow this wind back where it came from, gather these snowflakes together and wring them out until they were nothing but a bucket of harmless water drops.

And just as Willow is thinking this, the car's wheels begin to slide. Her mom slams on the brakes and the car slips—only a little at first, but then the ice suddenly shoots them sideways and sends them spinning. Around and around they go, like some wild carnival ride. Wisp slams into the side of the door because, of course, he didn't fasten his seat belt as he had promised he would. And their mom is fighting the car and the ice with all her gladiator strength.

And when their mom finally gets the car to stop, Willow can see they've hit something gray and solid, and she can feel the car tilting, like they're sitting on top of a giant seesaw. They are crosswise to the road, their front end low, their back end high. The car groans and slides slightly forward. Willow looks down, and through a sudden break in the mist and the snow, she sees water below them—swirling and rushing and splashing up toward their car as though trying to haul them all down to a watery grave.

But Willow says nothing, because in her family, you never, ever say the words "death" or "die" when Wisp is around.

CHAPTER 2

They hang suspended, as if time is no more and the world has stopped its spinning. There is nothing but silence. Willow senses the danger surrounding them in her glimpse of the water, in the tilt of the car, but she is not sure why they seem to be hanging in midair.

From the backseat, she hears the sound of her brother throwing up into the bucket they always bring for him.

"Wisp," Mom chokes out, "are you all right?"

"Yes," Wisp answers wearily.

"Should we get out?" Willow asks, and then notices that a line of blood is trickling down her mother's forehead.

"Mom!" she cries. "You're bleeding."

In the shock of the accident, Willow has not even considered whether any of them might have been hurt. Nothing *feels* broken or shattered to her.

Her mom puts a hand to her head and wipes the blood away. "It's all right," she says to both of them. "It's just a scratch. What about you, Willow?"

"I'm okay," Willow assures her mother.

The car lets out a groan, and for a moment, the snow lightens. And Willow sees what has happened. Their car is stuck on a metal bridge, and they are inches from going over the rails.

Before she can even let out the scream of terror that shrieks to be released, an angel appears through the wailing wind and slicing snow. The angel comes not on wings, but in warmth and lights. Two beams of a snowplow truck cut through the dark like a razor-sharp saw, and the roar of its engine breaks the silence of the storm and the inside of the car.

The back door on the high side of their vehicle is suddenly jerked open. Wind howls inside, bringing eye-burning cold and pelting snow and the sound of the river.

"Here now. Let's get you out of here quick," a grizzled face commands.

"Can you grab my son?" Mom says. "I think my daughter and I can get out by ourselves."

"I've got him," the old man assures her. "But don't you move. It's too dangerous. I'll be right back."

He lifts Wisp from the car and carries him away. They melt into the storm like ghosts disappearing through walls.

Willow hears the man call above the roar of blizzard and rushing waters. "We've got a minute more before she topples."

Willow's heart pounds in her ears at his words, and she lets out a soft moan. She does not want to be a dead almost-thirteen-year-old. There are too many things she hasn't done yet—gone

9

parasailing, ridden in a hot-air balloon, had cinnamon-cayenne ice cream.

"Willow?" Her mom's voice wobbles. "Can you free yourself?"

Willow reaches for her seat belt, and her frozen fingers undo the clasp. Her mom sighs at the sound of the click.

The car tilts slightly, and Willow's stomach lurches with it.

And then her door is yanked open, and a new face appears, a woman, all freckle-faced and honey-haired beneath her hat, her nose red with cold. "I'm here to take you out. Y'all just hold on."

"My journal," Willow says. Without thinking, she bends down and reaches for her precious notebook, which has fallen to the floor at her feet.

The car makes another awful metallic whine. Willow finally lets out that cry of terror she has been holding in, and even her mom whispers, "Dear God."

"Leave it, Willow," her mother adds through clenched teeth.

Willow obeys, unwilling to risk the move of a muscle.

The woman quickly puts an arm under Willow and lifts her out. The rushing waters thunder below them, and Willow sees just how precariously the car is balanced on this bridge that seems to have appeared out of nowhere.

"Mom!" she yells, struggling to free herself from this stranger, to bring her mother to safety too. But the woman has tightened her grip, as if she knew Willow would fight to go back to the tottering car to get her mother.

"He's got her, honey," the woman says to Willow. "Just look!"

And the man does. He has Willow's mom in his arms and has moved away from the car, when suddenly, everything gives way. Willow watches as the car topples front end first into the waters below. The crash of steel on rocks is a muffled explosion in the raging world of this storm.

Willow stands there until the snow and the strange silence in the aftermath of the crash remind her to breathe, because she realizes that for the last few minutes, she has been holding her breath.

"Wow," Wisp says into the quiet. "That was awesome."

CHAPTER 3

They all climb into the truck. As it moves forward, plowing through unending banks of snow, their rescuers introduce themselves. The man says his name is James McHenry. He is a local plowman, and the woman, Layla, is his wife. She knits in the dark as they drive. Her needles clack, clack, clack away, never once pausing. After Willow's mom introduces their family, James says he is taking them all to the town of Kismet, Maine, which is just a few miles down the road.

From the tiny backseat, Willow looks out the window as the windshield wipers fight a losing battle to clear the snow from the glass. They should be passing homes and shops, but truly, there is nothing to see in this whiteout world.

James and Layla chatter away, talking about the storm and how long they've been digging folks free. They marvel at how Willow's family got lost enough to wander so far from the main road and say they can't remember the last time someone came to town and crossed that bridge. The McHenrys are so chatty that not Willow, Wisp, or their mother can get a word in.

"Thirty years of marriage," James says, "and me and Layla still like being in this truck out in the snow, just the two of us, all warm and toasty with the cold outside our windows."

"All wrapped up together in a cocoon-like closeness," Layla agrees, and they smile at one another.

"Well, I'm grateful that you came along when you did," Mom finally manages to say. "I don't know what would have happened if you hadn't been there."

"Oh, no chance of that," Layla says, her laughter filling the truck. "Not in Kismet. We're always aware of any danger here."

The truck slows and then stops by a giant stone wall. In the glare of the headlights, a closed wooden gate appears. A sign— KISMET, MAINE, POP. 173—stands next to the invisible road.

James jumps out of the truck, his legs sinking deep into the snow. Willow expects to see him struggle to open the gate, to fight the mounds of moisture-laden flakes that have collected around it. He should need their help. But oddly, the gate opens easily after being unlocked, swinging on its hinges as if the ground were bare of any obstacle at all.

James is back in the truck in no time, moving it forward before getting out again to close the gate for good. It makes a loud thunking noise as it shuts.

They drive on until at last, Willow begins to see tiny twinkles of light. A few hundred yards more and the truck begins to climb a hill, groaning as it pushes ahead, bulldozing a path on the untraveled road. Snowflakes continue their madcap dance outside the windows, when suddenly, in front of them, a huge

13

Victorian house swims in and out of Willow's vision. The truck pulls up in front and comes to a stop.

"This is our town's bed-and-breakfast," James says. "Cora has a room for you tonight."

The B&B is massive, and shaped like an odd gingerbread house that someone seems to have added on to whenever the fancy took them without a care as to looks or function. It stands stark and dark against the snow-laden sky, all pointed angles and decorative trim.

James opens his door, steps down, and goes around the truck, opening the passenger side and reaching up to the front seat for his wife, who squeals at the cold and laughs as he lifts her out.

Willow pauses before following them, hesitant to leave the safety and warmth of this vehicle to head toward a building where she can almost imagine a wart-riddled witch might live. But her mom gives her a poke.

So Willow pushes the front seat forward and jumps down too.

Since they have no luggage, Willow and her mom hurry up the snow-filled walkway, helping Wisp along, as if propelled by the storm itself, toward the large inn. Their mom keeps a hand over Wisp's head, trying her best to keep the snow off his face.

As they get closer, Willow can see lace-curtained windows outlined by the lights inside. They soften the grim look of the house, promising warmth and shelter at last.

James and Layla don't bother knocking on the massive front door. They open it and shoo Willow's family inside. Soon they are all standing in a small hallway, complete with a coatrack and an umbrella stand. The walls are covered in rose wallpaper, and everywhere Willow can see, there are greens—long vines spiraling out of pots, broad leaves hanging lazily over couches, small trees gracefully scraping the ceiling.

"There you are," grunts a large woman with bright red lipstick and earrings that bobble as she rises from a chair in the living room. The chair looks as if a spider created it, all lines and curlicues and intricate wooden weaves. She meets them in the hallway.

"Here we are," James agrees. "Cora, meet Starr DuChard, her daughter, Willow, and her son, Wisp."

Cora gives them a brief nod, her eyes talon sharp upon them.

"We've got to get back to the plowing," James says to Willow's mom. "I'll stop by the local garage and let them know about your car, but I think they'll be too tied up at the moment dealing with this snow to do anything about it for a day or so."

"Oh, no. You don't have to bother," Mom protests. "I'll do it myself. We really can't wait that long. We have to get home as soon as possible—tomorrow morning at the latest. Is there a car rental agency around?"

James shakes his head. "Not for miles, I'm afraid. And this storm won't be letting up anytime soon."

"But it might," Mom says, and Willow can hear the determination in her voice. "Weather is unpredictable. It could clear."

Cora lets out a harrumphing sound, as if Willow's mom's hope is completely foolish.

"Either way, I'm afraid you're here for the night," James says. "Might as well make the best of it. Cora's beds are known to feel like heaven."

Cora smiles. "That they are."

Willow's mom nods absently, though Willow knows she is already worrying that they are so far from a real hospital and Wisp's doctors. She will not sleep tonight, fretting about Wisp, no matter how nice Cora's beds are.

"We're off, then," James says. "I'll check in on you all tomorrow." He smiles at Cora. "Sweet dreams."

"Sweet dreams," Layla echoes.

"You too," Cora says to them both.

James and Layla head out the door.

"Welcome to Kismet," Cora says, reaching to help them out of their coats, hanging them on the coatrack in the hall. "You can leave your winter gear right here. There's plenty of room. We don't get many visitors to our town."

"Do you live all alone in this place?" Wisp asks as he tugs off his boots.

"I certainly do," Cora tells him, waving them into her living room. The large common area has a fireplace and a window seat and comfortable-looking couches with needlepointed pillows thrown helter-skelter. Through an open doorway, Willow can see an enormous dining table. At the far end of the living room, there is a heavy dark wood reception desk with a window behind it that is pitch-black, a reminder to Willow of how far they are from cities and real civilization.

"Aren't you afraid some stranger will check in and rob you while you sleep?" Wisp asks.

Willow feels her face redden.

"Wisp," Mom scolds him.

But Cora just laughs, a hoarse chuckle that sounds as if she has spent a lifetime talking all day long. "Visitors aren't strangers once you get to know them, Wisp, and without even knowing you yet, I'd say you're not that strange either. Though now that I think on it, your name sure is odd. How'd you come to be called Wisp anyway?"

Wisp sighs with annoyance. It's a common question, one he hates.

But it makes their mom smile.

"His real name is Jack," Mom tells Cora. "But when he was little, he was always following his sister, Willow, everywhere she went. So his dad and I began to call him Will-o'-the-Wisp. And Willow was given her name because we wanted her to be like the tree: bendable in a strong wind but unbreakable, sturdy, with deep roots."

"Cute," the woman says, but Willow can see she isn't impressed with their mother's hippie-style of name-giving. Neither is Willow. She doesn't love her name.

"Well, your room is all ready for you upstairs," Cora adds.

The lines on her mom's face reappear, and her frown returns. "I'm afraid I don't have any money or credit cards to pay."

"Lost it all in the river," Cora says, nodding. Then she turns and shuffles away to lift a large brass key from a hook behind the reception desk. "Well, you can't leave here tonight, anyway. So not to worry. I expect I can get paid later, when we work everything out."

And it is at that moment that it suddenly dawns on Willow that, even though they are alive, they have lost everything—their car, Mom's wallet, their cash, their cell phones, which were charging in the car. Willow doesn't know how they will get home. Their dad could come get them, but that won't make their mom happy—Dad as rescuer rather than villain.

"Dad," Wisp whispers, as if reading his sister's thoughts. "Should we call him?"

Wisp has spoken soft and low, but their mom has heard. Her mom sucks in her breath. Anticipating a rant about their father, Willow turns away. She is about to make her mind think about the game again when she sees a line of seashells on one of Cora's windowsills. So instead, she concentrates on the sea smell of shells and how they can take you to the ocean even though they are often land-bound.

Then Willow feels sick to her stomach. She has remembered, in thinking of water, that she has also lost her journal. Willow prays that no one will find it floating down the river and read what she has written there—her most private thoughts, her personal daydreams, her darkest secrets. She begins to add up all that was in that car: her expensive hockey equipment and her computer. Anger and sorrow fill her, like baking soda and vinegar thrown together in a glass and about to fizz over. Willow doesn't know what to do about these feelings.

So she sucks in her breath, as her mom just did, and for a minute, it helps her feel a strange sense of peace. Suddenly, she understands why, in these past two years, her mom has been all small sighs and big breaths.

"We'll call your dad in the morning," Mom says. "It's too late now."

Cora walks back from the desk and hands Willow's mom the key. "Room's upstairs on the right. It's got a double bed there for you and your daughter, and I put a rollaway in for the boy."

Layla comes running in from outside. "Hey, y'all, I went and got these from the couple who own the drugstore. They're just the right size for each of you."

She holds up three sets of pajamas, three toothbrushes, and a tube of toothpaste in her pink perfectly manicured hands.

Willow sees her mom's anger and worry fade. It has been a long day, and her mom has obviously realized that there is nothing to do now but get some sleep and deal with everything in the morning. "Thank you. You've been wonderful."

"Well, that's what this town of Kismet is all about, missy," Cora says as Layla sings goodbye and heads back out into the storm.

Cora waves them toward the stairs. "Now off to bed with you. You three look like you could sleep standing up. Sweet dreams."

Obediently, they trudge up the stairs, passing black-and-white photos of a Kismet from long ago, people staring at the camera, mouths tight and unsmiling, their colorless seriousness giving Willow the creeps.

But when her mom opens the door to their room and they see the fluffy four-poster bed, and for Wisp, the little rollaway with a bucket nearby should he need it, they sigh and breathe, their bodies softening with release.

And it isn't until they are all in bed, and Mom's snores are washing over Willow as the snow washes over Cora's little B&B, that Wisp speaks out into the dark.

"How did that Cora lady know to bring in this extra bed and a bucket before we even got here?"

He's right, Willow thinks. *How in the world did she know?*

CHAPTER 4

Willow wakes at four a.m. She hears the chimes of a grandfather clock somewhere in Cora's house, marking the hour. Willow knows it was probably the deep booming of the gong that interrupted her sleep, but she might have woken up anyway. She is used to waking in the middle of the night.

Her father has trouble sleeping sometimes too. Some of Willow's best memories of him are of the two of them, sitting together on the front porch of their house in Vermont, in the deepest part of a summer night, whispering so they wouldn't wake Mom and Wisp. They'd talk about hockey or school or the basketball team her dad coaches until there was nothing more to say. Then they would just sit in the silence, looking up at the stars, or watching the fireflies flitting through Mom's organic garden until they were tired enough to go back to bed.

Sometimes, in the winter, her dad would make them both hot milk, and they'd sit in the kitchen drinking, with the cold pressing hard against the house. And when at last they were sleepy, he'd tousle Willow's hair and kiss her forehead and sometimes carry her back upstairs. Willow was eleven then, and thin as a pencil. Not like she is now—almost thirteen with older girl curves.

But those were what Willow calls the "before" days—before Wisp started getting occasional nosebleeds that wouldn't stop on their own and nausea and pains in his muscles, before the doctors told them they had no idea what disease Wisp might have, before their mom and dad fought over experimental treatments that forced their split.

Since her dad moved out a year ago, there have been no more of those talks and those silences, those mid-night minutes of closeness. And Willow still misses them when she wakes like this and just lies still, all alone in the night, her thoughts like restless sea waves. She wishes she were with her dad now, and she wonders if he's at his house, awake and wishing he could talk to her too.

Shivering, Willow gets up. Cora's house is cold, the wind seeping in through the cracks like fingers probing a purse for change.

Willow envies her best friend, Elise, right now. Elise and her sister and parents are on their way to spend the rest of the Christmas vacation in the Caribbean. Willow imagines Elise sleeping with her bedroom windows open, stars sprinkling the skies, a warm breeze blowing the curtains.

Willow knows the alarm that sits next to their bed, which

their mom set earlier, will go off in two hours. Her mom will hurry them into their clothes in the near dark and cold, anxious to leave here and get back home.

Shuffling to the window, Willow sees that the storm is still upon them, beating against the wooden houses of Kismet, Maine—big and little, one story and two. The storm they are enduring does not discriminate.

And she's thinking about her dad again, about the way his eyes crinkle when he laughs and the way he always sings Beatles songs in the shower. And she feels a surge of sadness that they are with him only on Tuesdays and Saturdays and hardly ever overnight because of Wisp's illness—when suddenly, Willow sees something strange.

As the wind blows and the snow parts, she catches a glimpse of Cora in the wan glow from the streetlights, bundled up and looking as huge as a sumo wrestler, waddling through the drifts and making her way down her drive to the unplowed road. She swings side to side, moving toward what looks like a lake with a large brick building at its end. Cora stops for a bit and then turns and lifts her head.

Willow freezes, for it's as if Cora is staring right up at her, as if she can see Willow standing there in the darkened room with the lace curtain pulled back, gazing down. Willow feels caught, as if she is spying on Cora.

But then Cora turns and continues. And Willow shakes herself. This is America—land of the free and home of the brave.

Standing here, watching out a window, is within her rights. Willow remembers her sixth-grade Revolutionary history lesson on freedoms.

So she stays there, and through the small breaks in the snowfall, she sees Cora unlock a door and go inside the large brick building. Then, in a last moment of clarity, before the storm gobbles up Willow's view for good, she sees that there is no one on the road anymore. It's just snow and emptiness again.

Willow stands there puzzled, until her feet are frozen into blocks of cold and her eyelids are heavy as ten-pound weights.

She makes her way back to the bed and slides in next to the heat of her mother. Willow lies there for a moment, thinking about what she has just seen.

Already, sleep is luring her back to unconsciousness. She yawns, unable to stay awake a moment more. Yet even as her eyes close, her thoughts are still swirling. *Why would Cora go outside in a snowstorm in the middle of the night? What is in that brick building that would make her brave all that snow?*

CHAPTER 5

The snow comes down as the sun comes up, showing no sign of whisking itself away. If anything, it has intensified, falling in slabs of white on the houses of Kismet, cloaking them in coats of thick cold. Trees bend under the weight. Power lines sag with possible outages.

"State of emergency's been declared over all New England. No one's allowed on the roads," Cora informs them as she pours Willow's mom a cup of coffee and puts a glass of orange juice in front of Wisp.

For a second, Willow thinks that maybe Cora has forgotten about giving Willow something to drink too.

"I'm getting yours," Cora says, as if reading Willow's mind. Willow stares at her in surprise.

Cora turns back to Willow's mom. "I'm afraid you're stuck here a few days more."

"But we need to get back," Mom says as she pulls at the napkin in her lap, lines forming at the sides of her mouth. "Maybe if I call the state and explain about Wisp, they'll make an exception."

"Won't," Cora says shortly. "Unless it's an emergency, no one's going anywhere."

"Is there a doctor in town?" Mom asks.

Cora nods. "Of course. Kismet may be small, but we have a hospital."

Mom sighs, looking over at Wisp. "I'll have to call in to work, I guess, and then I'll walk over to the hospital here just to check—in case we need them."

"I wouldn't worry about calling your office. No one is expecting anyone to go anywhere in this stuff," Cora says.

She heads into the kitchen and returns with a glass of grapefruit juice, plopping it down in front of Willow and giving her a wink. Willow's eyes widen. She loves anything with a tart, tangy taste that makes her tongue wince and reminds her brain with a jolt that she's alive: Sour Patch Kids, pickles, fresh lemonade—the more sour and explosive, the better. Willow was actually going to ask Cora if she had any grapefruit juice.

A strange tingling spirals down Willow's spine because it's as if Cora knew this. In fact, Cora seems to have a strange way of knowing lots of things. First there was the cot and the bucket, and now the juice. Willow can't shake a feeling that there is something uncanny about this woman—something peculiar. Then Willow remembers waking up and seeing Cora from the window.

"Last night, I saw you out in the storm, going down the road to a big brick building," Willow says.

Cora snorts but doesn't pause as she dishes steamy scram-

26

bled eggs onto their plates. "Now, missy, what would I be doing outside in this storm? You must have been dreaming."

"I wasn't dreaming," Willow argues. "I wake up in the middle of the night a lot. It was four a.m. I heard the clock. I was standing at the window watching the storm, and I saw you out there."

Cora lets loose a laugh so loud that Wisp and Willow and their mom all jump. "Girlie, there ain't no way you saw me outdoors in a snowstorm like we're having. I can barely make it up the stairs to my bed. How do you expect an old lady like me, with knees that can barely hold up a mosquito, to have stumbled her way through twenty-four inches of snow? You were dreaming, baby. It was nothing but a nice, big dream."

Maybe she was sleepwalking and sleep dreaming. But Willow doesn't think so. She remembers the solid feel of floor beneath her feet. So is she wrong or is Cora lying? And if she is lying, why?

Willow's mom eyes the eggs Cora has put in front of them. "Excuse me, Cora. You don't happen to have other breakfast choices, do you?"

DuChard *Spoken* Family Rule #1: Wisp is to eat nothing that is not organically grown. And since Wisp must follow this regimen, so must the entire DuChard family—without complaint.

Their dad disagreed with this decision. And so he is not there.

"This is a B&B, not a restaurant with a menu, and that

there is your breakfast," Cora says. "There's a storm going on, if you haven't noticed."

Willow can almost see her mom's thoughts wrestle each other: Should Wisp eat the eggs, even if the chickens that produced them probably weren't free-range, or should she stand firm and let him go hungry?

Obviously, there is no way of getting organic food in Kismet, Maine, in this blizzard. Eventually, their mom gives Wisp a nod.

Before she can change her mind, Wisp digs in enthusiastically. It has been months since he has eaten eggs that were obviously cooked in butter or bacon fat. His smile makes Willow smile too.

He shovels the eggs into his mouth with the speed of a freight train coming down the track. But then Willow sees him pause, and he sets his fork down quietly, his head drooping to his chest. She knows this is the signal that Wisp's stomach is rebelling. Silently, their mother moves his plate away and his bucket near.

Wisp swallows and swallows, until, at last, it seems the nausea has passed as he raises his head again. He looks at the eggs and sighs with frustration.

Tears prick their mother's eyes.

"Well, at least we've got power," Cora says, breaking the silence and awkwardness of the moment. "That's one thing to be thankful for. But now, see here. I do breakfast, not lunch or dinner. There's a diner down the street, and Mrs. Wallace, the owner, knows your situation. She's willing to let you eat there for free until you're able to get some money."

"Thank you," Mom says.

Cora pauses to spritz one of her plants. Its large leaves tremble with the touch of water, as if the gigantic bush is nodding in thanks.

"Do you think people who lose power will freeze to death in their homes before someone can reach them?" Wisp asks. "Will they be all stiff like ice cubes when they're finally found? Will their limbs break off when the police try to get them out?"

"Wisp," Mom sighs. "Please stop with the gory thoughts."

"Hello, hello," comes a loud voice from the hallway. A gust of cold tumbles into Cora's dining room.

A man comes in with the icy air. He is ramrod straight and military stern, with eyes set deep in a face that is lined and lean. In his hands, he carries a parcel wrapped in a plastic shopping bag.

"Colonel Stanley," Cora says, waddling forward to take the lanky man's coat and reaching up to brush the snow from his graying hair. "Glad to see you today."

"James and Layla are taking me around town," the colonel says, accepting a cup of hot coffee from Cora. "Being mayor and in charge of emergency services, I want to ensure that everyone is all right. You look like you have everything under control."

"I do, Colonel," Cora tells him, beaming. "As expected."

"Willow?" he barks at Willow, after he takes a sip of his drink.

"Yes," Willow says in surprise. How does he know her name?

"Layla asked me to give you this," he says, holding out a plastic bag.

Inside, Willow finds a spiral notebook, college lined, and a feathered ballpoint pen. She is a bit old for this type of pen, but already she can feel her fingers itching to write.

It was nice of Layla to have thought of this, and Willow gets it now. Layla has obviously told the colonel all about them. He is the mayor, after all.

"Have you been in a war?" Wisp asks, eyeing the colonel's uniform. "Have you fought in any really bloody battles?"

"Wisp!" Mom admonishes again.

The colonel nods. "Indeed I have, young man. Many years ago. Before I came here. But I prefer my life now to any battle-fields I've been on. Battles are usually unexpected. And I don't like being unprepared."

Wisp nods as if this is the most normal conversation ever. His fascination with gore and blood and war since the onset of his illness is one of the reasons Willow stopped having friends over—that and her mom and dad's increasing arguments over Wisp's treatment.

"Would you like to come along with me?" the colonel asks Wisp. "We could use a second lieutenant on our rounds."

Wisp beams, and the dark circles under his eyes seem to fade to light ash.

"No," Mom says, her voice like a shot going off in a metal room. "Wisp isn't well. I don't think the cold would do him good. But thank you for the offer."

DuChard *Spoken* Family Rule #2: Wisp is not to do anything that might weaken him further—no complaining.

Their dad put up a bit of a fight about babying Wisp. And so he is not here.

Willow watches Wisp wilt.

"Well." The colonel pauses for a few seconds, eyeing Wisp. "If that's the final decision . . ."

And you can feel the colonel's question hanging like smoke in the air.

But Wisp doesn't have the strength these days to continually fight their mom.

He looks down at his lap. His shoulders sag. He whispers, "We'd probably go over a cliff or something out there anyway. We'd probably die in a fireball of explosions."

The colonel waits another second, but when Wisp says nothing more, he nods and shrugs back on his wool overcoat, handing Cora his cup. "I'm off, then. Thanks for the coffee, Cora."

The man goes out, taking the cold with him.

Willow can see Wisp's disappointment in the bend of his back. Her heart gives a sad little swish.

Their mom stands. "I'm going to try to reach work anyway, and I should call your father and let him know where we are. Let him know we're okay, although *as usual,* he won't be any help."

Willow quickly glances around the room to find something to think about, to block out more of her mother's wearisome grievances about their dad. And she sees some books in a book-case and makes herself think about Dr. Seuss, whose books she truly adored when she was younger. Willow loved how he always tried to simplify life, even in a seriously complicated world. Finally, her mom says no more and leaves the room, taking her bitterness with her.

Willow wishes she could call her best friend, tell her all about the situation they are in, but Willow has no cell phone now. And, of course, Elise is almost two thousand miles away in a foreign country, probably sunning on a beach.

"Wisp," Cora says, all brisk business now, "how about you help me carry these dishes in? Willow, why don't you get the door?"

Puzzled, Willow looks at Cora. But then a hard knock sounds.

Staring at the door, Willow wonders how Cora could possibly have known that someone was coming. She turns back toward Cora, but Cora is already heading to the kitchen.

Willow looks at Wisp, who shrugs. And so she goes and opens the door.

Standing before her is the oddest-looking boy she has ever seen.

CHAPTER 6

He is a mishmash of contrasts. One blue eye and one green—as if God could not decide whether this boy should see the world through sky or leaves. On one foot is an L.L.Bean fishing boot and on the other a plain brown work boot. One black mitten and one red glove shower down snow as he takes them off. Willow stares.

He grins at her. "Hi, Willow. I'm Topher Dawson."

He holds out his hand, and Willow looks first before touching him. Will he be fingerless on one hand and six-fingered on the other? But he seems to have normal limbs and all ten fingers.

Willow shakes his hand, and cold and snow scent the air around him.

He removes his hat, and the contrasts continue. Thick, dark hair tickles his neck. One feather-braided streak of green decorates the left side. His blue-green eyes move past her.

"And you must be Wisp," he says, kicking off his boots. His socks, predictably, don't match either.

33

Wisp has come in from the kitchen and is hanging back, staring shyly at the boy before him.

Topher swings a backpack off his shoulder. "Layla said you guys were holed up here. Thought you might like to hang out, play a game or something."

He pulls Life from his bag, and Willow sees Wisp's face light up with delight.

"I love that game," Wisp says.

"Me too," Topher says. "Come on, then. Let's set it up. My brothers will be along in a minute to join us."

As if on cue, Cora comes back from the kitchen. "Hello, Topher."

"Hey, Cora," Topher says.

"Come to entertain my guests?" she asks as she moves about the room, adding fertilizer to one of her plants before snapping off a dead leaf.

Topher laughs. "Them and my own hooligan little brothers. Mom's busy at the hospital."

"How many brothers do you have?" Wisp asks. "Are any of them sick?"

Willow sucks in her breath at her brother's inappropriate question.

Topher looks thoughtful. "Uh, nope. I don't think so. They were both healthy when I left them ten minutes ago. Too healthy, really," he adds. "They *never* slow down."

His eyes rest on Willow for a minute, as if she can empathize. But Willow can't. She would give the sun and the moon to have Wisp wear her out.

"Joe Joe is twelve, and Taddie is eight," Topher says.

"That's my age!" Wisp shouts, pumping a fist in the air.

"Are you a wild loup-garou like my brothers?" Topher asks, laughing.

"What's a loup-garou?" Willow can't help but ask. She's never heard the word before.

He turns to her. "It's a kind of wolf, a wolf who is always causing trouble in our Acadian folk stories."

"Are you French Canadian?" Willow asks.

Cora laughs, that loud laugh that makes Wisp and Willow jump again. "Almost everyone in town is. Our ancestors made their way here years ago, seeking a different kind of life. But we're descended from the original settlers up there—loggers, fiddlers, and farmers, every one."

Topher shrugs. "I'm only half, though."

He gives Willow a look with his peculiar eyes. "My mother is Acadian, but my father was from away."

Away? Willow thinks that an odd choice of words.

"Was?" Wisp asks, picking up on another of Topher's words. "Is your dad dead?"

Topher shakes his head. "No, my parents are divorced. My dad doesn't live here anymore. He didn't like living in Kismet."

"Why not?" Wisp asks.

Topher shrugs. "Too many people knowing everyone's business is what he thought."

"Does he visit you often?" Wisp asks.

"No . . . ," Topher says slowly. "He never visits."

"Doesn't he like you?" Wisp asks.

"Wisp!" Willow protests again.

But Topher just laughs as he sits down and begins to set up the game board on the dining room table. "He likes us well enough. It's Kismet he's not fond of. And actually, he isn't allowed to visit."

Cora coughs loudly, and Topher's eyes swing toward hers. Cora gives him an odd look, and Willow sees Topher redden.

"Why isn't he allowed to visit?" Wisp asks, his bold curiosity insatiable.

"Because that's what Topher's mom and dad agreed on," Cora interrupts sharply. "Right, Topher?"

Topher nods but says nothing else. He gazes down at the floor.

Willow thinks of her own dad and how little her mom wants him around now too.

"Do you miss him?" Wisp asks softly, walking over and leaning his body into Topher's knee.

Topher places a palm on Wisp's head. He looks right at Wisp. "I miss him every day."

Willow wonders at Topher's ability to speak so calmly of this. He does not blink back a tear. His voice does not waver.

He is like those settlers of bygone days whom Willow has read about—rugged and tough.

Topher may be settler strong, but Willow thinks of her own dad again and a lump lodges hard in her throat.

Cora nods as if satisfied before heading into the kitchen.

Topher glances behind him, and then leans toward Willow and Wisp. In a voice so soft that only they could possibly hear, he says, "My dad would visit if he could. But there's a reason he can't. It's a secret."

Wisp's eyes widen. His mouth opens, but before he can say anything, Topher puts a finger to his lips. "Please don't ask. I'm not allowed to tell you why—not today, anyway."

Wisp nods solemnly, thrilled, Willow can tell, to share a confidence with an older boy. But Willow just feels baffled. What could possibly be so top-secret about his father not visiting?

"Your family plans on leaving as soon as you can, right?" Topher asks, an odd sense of what Willow identifies as urgency in his voice.

"Yes," she says. "Why?"

Topher glances behind him again. "Because you don't want to stay here. Believe me."

Before Willow can ask why again, a storm of arms and legs and giggles and shouting descends on them all.

Topher's brothers arrive in a flurry of coats and boots and mismatched mittens. But unlike Topher's, all four of their eyes are river-bottom brown, and their hair is cut straight and true and just below their ears.

"Ah, Topher," the older one says. "Not Life again! Can't we go sledding or have a snowball fight instead?"

"Quiet!" Cora comes back into the room and shouts into the uproar, and her voice, like her laugh, boomerangs off the walls. "You ruffians may stay in my house, but put a lid on the noise."

The boys grow quiet immediately.

"Now, you want hot chocolate, I take it," Cora says as they settle down.

"Yes, please!" the boys yell.

Then each of them eyes Cora guiltily, but she just laughs. "Hot chocolate, already made and coming up."

Willow watches Cora waddle off again toward the kitchen. Then she turns back to Topher, planning on asking him about his dad and why they should be worried about staying in Kismet.

But Topher shakes his head at her.

Willow crosses her arms in irritation. Why won't he tell them?

She decides then and there to ignore this boy and his silly, probably stupid secret and ominous warning. After all, it's not as if she will be around after today. They *are* leaving.

"Taddie, Joe Joe," Topher says, introducing his brothers, and pointing to each, "this is Wisp and Willow."

Taddie is shorter than Joe Joe by about two inches. Like

Wisp's, his eyes shimmer with mischief, and his lips threaten laughter. Joe Joe stands beside his brother, taller and gawky, with a few pimples.

"Hey," they say to Willow and Wisp.

"Okay, come on, then. Game time," Topher says. "What color car do you each want to be?"

"I want green!" Taddie shouts.

"Can't we play anything else? How about hearts?" Joe Joe asks, continuing his plea to do something different.

"Wisp likes Life," Topher says. "So Life it is."

"I like Life too," Taddie says. Wisp and Taddie exchange excited looks, and Willow can tell that all thoughts of secrets have left Wisp's head in the face of a possible new friendship.

"Fine," Joe Joe relents. "I'll be whatever color."

"Willow?" Topher says. "What color car do you want to be?"

He looks at Willow with his odd-hued eyes, his gaze open, waiting.

"I think I'll pass," Willow says.

"Really?" Topher asks, his eyebrows raised.

His look gives her a funky feeling, a rumbling, tumbling jolt of something Willow cannot describe. It is an odd feeling, just like him.

"I don't like playing games with Willow." Wisp suddenly speaks up, breaking this boy's spell. "She's a brainiac. She won the school geography contest last year and is the highest scorer on her school's debate team and has read more books than the librarian at my school." He rolls his eyes as if to emphasize his point.

Willow sticks her tongue out at her brother, and Wisp laughs and sticks his tongue back out at her. It is their weird little ritual, this tongue-sticking-out, something their parents taught them to do years ago to stop them from using their fists when they were angry with each other. It has always made them laugh so their differences disappear, and today is no exception.

Cora comes in with mugs of dark chocolate, clouds billowing from the cups like trains in a station enveloped in their own steam.

The boys giggle and laugh. And Willow sees that Wisp is now acting like a bit of a wild frontiersman himself, easily joining in the merriment of Topher and his brothers. Without Willow, the game begins, and Willow is released to do what she wants.

She goes to the window seat near the front of the house. Down the road, she sees someone trudging along with his head down, fighting his way through the snow, hands stuck deep in the pockets of a bright red parka. He turns a corner and goes inside the brick building Willow saw last night. She wonders again about seeing Cora out there, and what must be inside that building, before she turns her thoughts to her writing.

She opens the notebook Layla has sent as Cora comes and sets a mug of chocolate near her. If Willow cannot be with Elise, she will spend time with her nonhuman friend, the blank page. The scent of new paper rises to melt with the steam of the drink, and the view of the snow outside and the feel of the warmth inside prickle with peace. Soon Willow is writing, lost in words and thoughts, all flowing onto the pages as if a tap has finally been unclogged. Mud and sludge spill out.

Willow has always loved the play of written words and the sound of them in her mouth, especially big words, rare words, words people hardly ever use, words that can change lives or minds. But since Wisp took ill, her writing seems to only be about sad and ugly things. She knows her tales now would horrify her parents, but sometimes making up tragic stories is the only thing that keeps her from worrying about Wisp or the separation of her mom and dad.

Time passes, and Willow continues writing.

And then she is taken away from her quiet reverie by a rise in voices. Life has become a winner-take-all contest, a race to the finish.

Willow stands up and moves toward the large wooden dining room table. It is Wisp's turn, and he spins the wheel just as Joe Joe and Taddie begin arguing over who owes what to whom. Wisp is distracted, listening to them, and Willow watches as Topher slyly reaches out and swings the wheel just slightly to the left, adding a two-space advantage to Wisp's roll.

"Boys," Topher says, his voice steady and stern. "Your arguments are pointless. Wisp has won."

"I have?" Wisp cries, turning to look at the board. "I have!" he shouts in triumph as he realizes the number on the wheel places him over the finish line.

Topher's eyes meet Willow's, and there is a light dancing behind them, turning one eye Easter-egg blue and the other spring-grass green. He shrugs innocently with open palms, as if he had no choice but to pull this trick.

In spite of herself, Willow feels a smile break free on her face.

This boy with green-streaked hair and mismatched eyes may be strange, but how is it possible to dislike a boy who cheats at Life to let Wisp win?

CHAPTER 7

Willow's mother comes into the room, her eyes red-rimmed and her lids rubbed raw. And Willow realizes in a flash that her mom has not just phoned work to say she would not be there or spoken to their dad or made the phone calls to get them out of this town.

Her mother's face betrays the fact that she has also called the doctors and gotten the results of a test Wisp took before they left for Canada. Willow knows the look. She's seen it on her mother's face many times before. The last test must have been negative, leaving them, once again, unsure as to what is wrong with Wisp.

"What is going on in here?" Mom asks, quickly bringing down her mother mask, as she often does, clearly shoving Wisp's test results deep into the back of her brain.

"I just won Life!" Wisp says.

Mom blinks in surprise, but she recovers quickly. Her fingers graze the bangs that hang low in Wisp's eyes. "Did you, Wisp? That's wonderful."

Topher stands and holds out a hand. "Topher Dawson, ma'am. Boys?" he adds, and obediently his brothers stand too. "My brothers, Taddie and Joe Joe." Topher points to each.

They all shake her mom's hand sweetly and seriously, and her mom smiles. The Dawsons are winning her over with an ease that irritates Willow.

Topher begins to gather up the board. "We have to go. My mom'll be home from the hospital soon."

"Your mother's a doctor?" Willow's mom asks.

"She's the best one ever," Taddie brags.

"Their mother is Acadian—that means French Canadian," Wisp bursts out, grinning at his new friends. "Everybody here is."

"I'm only half," Topher reminds him, "though my mom is full Acadian."

"She can cure anything," Joe Joe adds.

"She took care of my bunions," Cora says as she comes down the stairs from carrying up clean towels. In her hand, she has a box of beads and a long string of wire. She eases herself into the deep, flowery sofa, yelping as her knees give in. She pours the beads out onto a dark wooden butler table with a rim that catches the balls and prevents them from spilling onto the floor. "And she brought the colonel through a bad bout of pneumonia last winter. The boy's right. She's a healer."

"A healer?" Mom asks, and Willow winces.

Her mom's face falls into speculation. And Willow sees a spark of hope in her eyes. In the same flash, she can see her father's frown and hear his voice with all its disapproval.

44

"Don't, Starr," he would say. "Let it go."

But he's not here, and Willow knows her mom won't. Over and over the doctors have told her mother that only Wisp's body can beat this thing—but her mom keeps pushing to find the one doctor who can figure out the truth and come up with a cure.

DuChard *Unspoken* Family Rule #4: Never give up on Wisp—even if it kills everyone else.

In that moment, Willow almost hates this boy, Topher Dawson. Her mom is going to want to meet his mom to get her opinion on Wisp. Willow knows it.

Topher returns the game to his backpack. He and his brothers plunge once more into their coats and boots and mittens and gloves.

"See you tomorrow?" Taddie asks Wisp.

"We're heading home later today," Willow says quickly, hoping to stop her mother from trying to track down Topher's healer mom.

"Oh, you'll be here," Cora says. "Ain't no one going nowhere in this weather." Her fingers shuffle through the tiny glass globes.

"What are you making?" Wisp asks, curiosity drawing him nearer.

Cora pulls down the collar of her shirt to reveal a beaded necklace circling a wrinkled neck. Each bead is etched with a leaf. "I sell them at the fair in the summer."

"Cora's a real *artist*," Topher says.

He grins at Willow as if this is a joke they can share. And perhaps he's right. Willow can easily tell that Cora's handiwork is not exceptional, though her ability to grow plants is obviously amazing. They are taller and greener than any plants Willow has ever seen.

But Willow does not return Topher's open smile. This boy may have kindled a flame in her mother's heart, giving her false hope once more.

"See you later, Willow," Topher calls as he heads for the door, his playful, tumbling puppy brothers crowding around him as they head off into the snow-whiteness.

But Willow says nothing. Instead, she watches her mother, who stands there, staring after the boys.

Suddenly, her mother grabs her coat, puts it on, and moves toward the door. Willow knows where she is headed.

"I don't think Taddie meant his mother was a miracle worker," Willow says, hurrying after her mom, wanting to end this crusade before it begins.

"Willow, what kind of mother would I be if I didn't at least talk to her?" her mother asks.

Willow says nothing, for there is no good response to this question. She watches the front door open and then close behind her mom. And once again, Willow is left standing alone in her mother's wake as her mother sails off in search of a cure for Wisp.

CHAPTER 8

Willow sits in a chair by the window, watching the snow as it continues to fall, each flake adding to the already mountainous heaps of white. For a minute, the sun forces its way through sinister-looking clouds and shines and shimmers on the town, making her squint. And then it is gone again, swallowed whole by stormy intentions.

Down the street, James McHenry's plow moves slowly into driveways, pushing snow back and forth, until Willow begins to see how each person's driveway was connected to the main road before snow reshaped the town's world.

Kismet itself is small. From Cora's B&B on the hill at one end, Willow can see all the way to the other. Every structure except one is made of wood—fine planked, straight and tight—and each house is part of a cul-de-sac, each cul-de-sac running off the main street. Not many homes, except Cora's and a few others, are more than one story tall. Willow sees the big brick building, along with a drugstore and a library, a post office and a bank, the diner and a tiny movie theater, and far down the road, the hospital, a grocery store, a school, a police station, and a gas station. That is all there is to Kismet, Maine.

When the plow arrives in front of Cora's, Willow sees Layla in the front seat. Through the window, Willow holds up the journal and mouths "Thank you." Layla gives her a grin and a nod, her knitting needles never stopping.

Then they are gone, back out onto the streets, weaving their way through Kismet, creating pathways and trails through which the townspeople can find their way in this newly formed and unfamiliar landscape. As the plow moves on, Willow notices for the first time that the streets of Kismet are oddly bare. There are no mailboxes on the road or on porches, no newspaper boxes or doors with mail slots. Where does the mailman put the mail?

Cora has turned on a gas fire, and the flames flicker and flash. Willow's mom has been gone all afternoon.

Willow's dad calls around five on Cora's house phone since their cell phones are at the bottom of whooshing waters bound for lakes or rivers or oceans. Willow answers eagerly, but her dad sounds strained and worried.

"I talked to your mom this morning," he says, "but I'm glad to be talking to you now. Are you all right? How is Wisp? I wanted to come get you, but the state of emergency is keeping everyone off the roads."

Willow tells him that they are both okay, that they will see him in a day or two when everything clears. She does not mention where her mom has gone. There would be little her father could do anyway about her mother's crusade, and Willow is still hoping that nothing will come of it.

When Willow goes back to the living room, Cora continues to work, her hands stringing bauble after bauble into a merry string of greens and golds. The sound of one bead clacking against another as it is threaded and dropped is somehow comforting.

Wisp has fallen asleep. His head rests lazily on the sofa cushions. His woolen-socked feet have found a way to nestle in Cora's large lap, and Cora has laid a blanket over him.

Willow looks back out the window and sees two people trudging through the snow toward the brick building. They disappear inside.

"Come away from the window, girl," Cora says. "It's cold there, and you can't change a thing."

"What?" Willow asks, even as she stands up and moves over to Cora.

Cora shrugs. "Your mother is a grown woman and is quite safe. Not everything is your responsibility, you know."

"What do you mean by that?" Willow asks.

Cora doesn't answer. Instead, she nods her head toward Wisp. "What's wrong with him?" Her voice, usually booming and banging, now slides softly through the warm room like heated taffy poured out of a hot pan.

"They don't know," Willow says. "They've tried test after test and treatment after treatment, and they can't figure it out."

Willow pauses and then raises her eyes to meet Cora's. "I heard one time . . . because my parents didn't know I was outside their bedroom . . . I heard my dad say the doctors told him there was a possibility that Wisp could even die."

This is a moment Willow tries to forget, so she's not sure why she's told this woman about it. She has never told anyone else what she's learned.

"Nobody promised you fair when you came into this world, girl," Cora says. "And nobody promises you fair on how or when you go out. The best you can do is to be prepared."

Willow sits down and hands Cora a bead.

"I hate him being sick," Willow whispers.

Cora's hand shoots out and envelops Willow's before she can pull it away. Willow can feel the lines and creases of Cora's palm, its worn spots and soft spots.

"I know," Cora says. "But you can relax for now. He'll be okay today."

Willow stares at her. There is no way for Cora to know how Wisp will feel for the rest of the day. Even Willow can't predict how Wisp will be hour to hour, and she lives with him and his illness all the time. Why would this woman say such a foolish thing?

Before she can ask Cora what she means, the front door opens, and Willow's mom comes in from the cold. Snowflakes lie on her coat, hat, and mittens, evidence that she has been braving the snow for quite some time. Willow takes one look at her mom's face and sees disappointment there.

"I tried to follow those boys," her mom says as she takes off her coat, "but I couldn't find them. I walked around and around the town, but the snow covered their tracks too quickly. So I went to the hospital, but their mother was gone for the day. The staff wouldn't give me their address. The only good that came from all this was confirming that Wisp's doctors have sent his records here. I spent a few hours getting all the paperwork done so they'll be ready if we need them."

Willow suppresses a sigh of relief. For now, Wisp is free from any new treatments.

"Can you tell me how to get to the Dawsons' house?" Mom asks Cora.

"Tomorrow," Cora says. She gently picks up Wisp's feet and lays them to the side, then pushes her heavy frame from sitting to standing. "You should have an early supper at the diner tonight. There's a lull now, but there's more heavy snow coming this evening."

Willow sees her mom start to protest, but then Wisp stirs, and their mom is at his side, her hand on his too-skinny arm, her mind completely focused on her son. Wisp opens one eye and then pulls his arm away from his mother.

"I'm hungry," he says.

Willow is hungry too, realizing only now that they have had breakfast but no lunch. It's five-thirty, but her stomach must think it's seven-thirty, the way it is groaning and growling.

The idea of going outside shimmers like freedom. Willow is suddenly longing to escape this cooped-up, waiting world they have been in all day.

Their mom eyes Wisp uncertainly. "Maybe Willow and I should go alone. We could bring you something back."

"I *want* to go," Wisp whines, sitting up.

Already, Willow can see the defeat in his eyes.

"He's been inside all day, Mom," Willow says, coming to her brother's defense. "And he slept."

Her mother thinks for a moment, and Willow can see her begin to bend.

"He slept for two hours while you were gone," Willow tells her.

Please let him go, she thinks. *Please.*

"All right then," her mother says at last. "Get dressed."

As quickly as air shoots out of a popped balloon, Wisp is up, and he and Willow pile on hats and mittens, boots and coats.

"Would you like us to bring you something?" Mom asks Cora.

Cora nods. "That would be nice. I've some watering to do here. Now, Old Woman Wallace makes good meat loaf. No veggies. I hate veggies. I'll be here when you get back, with the fire going. I appreciate you helping a tired lady out. That snow would be too much for me and my knees."

Willow is reminded again of last night and of seeing Cora walking down the snow-covered street. If Cora won't go out for food, why would she go out at four in the morning for no good reason? Willow *must* have been dreaming.

And then they are off—out into a world gone white and wild. Wisp tugs on Willow's arm and begs her to race him. And so they run, slipping and sliding along. Wisp hoots and hollers all the way there.

Before Wisp got sick, he too played hockey, and he skied. Their dad called him his little daredevil, as Wisp was always taking the kinds of chances that made their mom and dad go white with worry.

Willow loves that her brother is racing her now, sliding when he can in his boots, laughing and snorting.

"Careful," Mom calls to them. "Slow down, Wisp."

DuChard *Unspoken* Family Rule #5: Wisp must be careful at all costs.

And so they slow down, but they do not cease their play. And their laughter echoes in the silent streets, like rumbling thunder through snow-sodden hills.

Soon, though, the diner rises out of the white piles of snow, ending their brief tumble back into carefree. A neon sign flashes a welcome in the dark, merrily lighting the front door.

Their mother shoos them inside.

The heat of the diner rises like a wall against Willow's nose. She unties her scarf, pulls off her mittens. Wisp does the same, the color on his cheeks red-rosy and bright.

"Sit wherever you want," a waitress calls to them. She heads over. "Oh, and you'll need these." She hands them each a menu, crisp and seemingly brand-new.

The place is packed, but it's cozy, with a "come on in and join us" kind of noise, and so they slide into a booth with red leather seats. On the wall beside them is an old-fashioned jukebox. Willow spins the dial but doesn't recognize any of the songs, though she knows the singers: Elvis Presley, Dean Martin, Frank Sinatra—singers her grandparents used to listen to, songs from the past for this backwoods town.

"I want a hamburger," Wisp says as he looks over the menu.

Their mom shakes her head. "The eggs were enough, Wisp. Let's see if we can't find something healthy to eat."

Wisp scowls. A glance at the menu tells Willow that he will win this round. There is nothing here for a tofu-loving, organic-vegetable eater. Meat loaf, mac and cheese, hamburgers and fries—these are all that are available.

Willow looks over at the other tables and notices that no one else has menus. They are simply ordering, as if they know the food by heart. And though it seems strange, perhaps they do. There probably is no other place to eat in Kismet. Over time, maybe they have memorized everything.

"May I take your order, fair lady?"

Willow looks up to see a pair of mismatched eyes meeting hers, a boy in a Wallace Diner shirt—the boy with a secret. Topher grins.

CHAPTER 9

"You work here?" Willow asks before she can stop herself. If she is to get rid of this boy who seems to simmer with goodwill and who offers her mom false hope, Willow must remember not to give an inch, or, she can tell, this boy will take a mile.

"Sometimes," Topher says. "My cousin owns the place, so I get called in if they need help. Just for an hour or two, though. I'm too young to get paid, but I can eat whatever I want."

Willow's mom eyes him. "I tried to find you after you left. I'd like to talk to your mom. Can you give me her number?"

"She doesn't have a phone," Topher says.

"No cell phone?" Willow's mom asks, her eyes screwed up, puzzled.

In spite of herself, Willow too is curious. She has never heard of a doctor without one.

"No one in Kismet has a cell phone," Topher says, shrugging.

Willow looks at him in shock. "No one?"

Topher shakes his head.

"Why not?" Willow asks. Most of her friends have cell phones, and she's never heard of an adult not having one.

"Never needed one," Topher says.

"So you just have landlines?" Willow asks, mulling over this odd fact.

"Not even those, really," Topher says. "The only one in town is at Cora's B&B."

"That's kind of quaint," Willow's mother says. "I guess in a town this small, you don't need them much, right?"

"But what if you have a problem?" Willow asks, still stumped by this strangeness. "What if you're stuck somewhere and need help?"

"Someone always finds you," Topher says with confidence. "Layla and James found you, didn't they?"

Willow isn't sure how to respond to this. While it's true that they were found, it is also possible that they wouldn't have been. And then what would have happened? Willow shivers. She doesn't want to ever think again about the car tilting on the bridge that night and the rushing waters below them.

Topher turns to Willow's mother. "Not to worry. My mom is usually free at the hospital by lunch, after she's done rounds. You'll find her there tomorrow if you want."

Willow's mom nods her thanks, and Willow is once again wishing for a sudden rise in temperature, a horrific spurt to ninety degrees, so all this whiteness would wash clean away and Wisp could run from needles and health shakes and pills.

"How old *are* you?" Wisp asks. "Are you old enough to go to war and get shot?"

Willow blushes.

DuChard *Unspoken* Family Rule #6: If you are sick, you can ask anyone anything you want.

Wisp takes full advantage of this rule.

Topher laughs. "I know I'm tall for my age, Wisp. But I'm only twelve. And even though I'll be thirteen in a few days, I don't think a war is in my immediate future. Hey," he adds, "if you're still in town on my birthday, you could celebrate with me."

"Can I, Mom?" Wisp cries.

"We won't be here, Wisp. We've got to get you home," Mom says. Then she turns to Topher. "Do you have any soup? Maybe vegetable soup?"

Their mom is nothing if not persistent.

"We have chili," Topher says. "And really great nachos. And Mrs. Wallace makes the best hamburgers, gooey with cheese."

Their mom sighs.

"I want an Old Woman Wallace hamburger," Wisp says, using Cora's name for the owner of the café, and then sitting back and crossing his arms, his lips pressed tight, a small act of defiance he hasn't attempted in months.

Their mom ignores him.

"Don't call her Old Woman Wallace if she's around and can hear you," Topher says, raising an eyebrow and nodding toward the back of the restaurant. "And believe me, she knows and hears everything going on in this place!"

In the window of the kitchen, Willow sees a woman moving around. She is not young, but her eyes seem needle sharp. And her arms look weight-lifter strong.

"Order!" Old Woman Wallace barks. Her voice is deep and gruff, almost angry.

"Will she spit in my drink?" Wisp asks, his eyes wide as he watches Mrs. Wallace command her kitchen. "Will she put poison in my food?"

"Don't be stupid, Wisp," Willow says. "She can't hear you from way over there. There's no way she would know what you just called her."

She gives Topher her best withering glance, but Topher leans over the booth until his face is close to Willow's.

"Actually, she might," he says softly.

Willow rolls her eyes. "How? Or is this another secret of yours?"

"Nope," Topher says, and his voice is sad. "Same one."

"Well, what is it?" Willow challenges him.

"You have to be part of the town to know, and I really hope you don't stay and find out," Topher whispers. "I want you to go home."

Willow leans away from him. Of course she's going home—as soon as possible! Willow wants to get back to her dad and her friends, and her mom certainly wants to get back to Wisp's doctors. Still, this boy is almost rude in his desire to have her leave.

"You don't need to worry," Willow finally snaps at him. "We're going as soon as the snow clears. We wouldn't want to live in this old town anyway."

"Good," Topher says. Then he stands back up and lets out a sigh of what seems to be relief.

Willow is baffled. Why does he seem so determined to get them out of town? Does he not like them? He didn't have to come over to play a game with them this morning. She certainly didn't ask him over.

But he's gazing at her with kind eyes, not spiteful ones. Willow stares back at him, truly puzzled and trying to pretend she doesn't feel that same strange fluttery feeling deep in her stomach she felt earlier when he looked at her. And though she is struggling not to, she has to admit she is a little curious now about this secret Topher keeps hinting at—the reason his father isn't able to visit, the way Old Woman Wallace knows everything that goes on in the restaurant. Could the secret be something really worth knowing? Or is he just playing with them? And why do they have to be part of the town to know it? The whole thing sounds like a joke to Willow.

Their mother closes the plastic menu with a sharp slap, and Willow is brought back to reality. "Fine. There doesn't seem to be much choice here. Order what you want. But, Wisp, you are back on a healthy diet as soon as we leave here tomorrow."

Topher straightens and goes behind their mom. He grins and gives Wisp a V sign with his fingers.

Wisp looks at Willow. "Peace?"

"Victory," Willow whispers in his ear, smiling just a bit. It is kind of funny—even if this boy *is* annoying.

Wisp turns his head, hiding his grin from their mom.

CHAPTER 10

The plates come to their table in minutes, steaming hot and dripping with oil and cheese. Willow stares in surprise as Topher puts the plates down.

"Wow, that was quick," Willow's mom says.

That is exactly what Willow was thinking.

Topher shrugs. "Yeah, some people say Mrs. Wallace is a mind reader, she cooks orders so fast."

He gives Willow that same odd look, as if this should mean something to her. Is he implying that the older woman is telepathic? The idea is absurd.

"Well, enjoy," he says, and then he's off to help other customers.

Willow watches him go, and then the smell of the food hits her. Her mouth waters. She turns back to her plate and digs in. Both she and Wisp gobble up most of their dinner. Surprisingly, their mom, after she has poked her BLT with a fork, doesn't leave even one bite on her plate either.

Layla arrives and pulls a chair up to their booth. "Hey, y'all. I see you're getting along okay."

She has on a large furry coat that steams with melting snow. Her blond hair is piled high and her sparkly earrings catch the light of the diner.

"We're fine," Mom says. "And we really can't thank you enough for all you've done. Getting us out of that car, driving us to Cora's."

Layla laughs. "It was nothing, honey. Glad to do it. Me and James are just taking a break. The snow's quit for an hour, so we need to eat fast and get what we can cleared out."

"You must be exhausted," Mom says.

"Oh no, honey," Layla says. "Me and James are always prepared. Why, we can go whole hog on just forty winks. How's your writing coming, sweetie?" Her eyes rest on Willow.

"Thanks for getting me the journal," Willow says.

Layla grins. "Well, baby, if you write about Kismet, make sure I'm a star in your story."

Willow's stories are not star-studded. They are more grease and grime.

"Maybe someday you'll be famous like that Harry Potter writer," Layla says, winking at Willow. "Someone told me she's richer than the queen of England. Isn't that the dream?"

Willow shrugs. Lately her only dream is of her brother recovering and her parents getting back together. Any other kind of future doesn't really seem to matter.

Layla turns to Wisp. "Heard you were the hero of the match today."

"I won Life," Wisp says.

Layla laughs. "Of course you did."

Willow is about to ask Layla who told her about Wisp and the game and how she knew he won, but then Layla looks up and Willow sees that James is in the doorway, an overstuffed paper bag in his hand.

"Gotta run," Layla says. "See y'all real soon."

And she is gone before a word has left Willow's mouth.

The door opens a minute later with a whoosh of wind, and the colonel steps jauntily into the diner. He is wearing a grin from ear to ear and handing out cigars to some of the men in the diner.

"Colonel Stanley!" Wisp cries. "Did you find dead people buried under all the snow? Were they white and slimy?"

The colonel walks toward them, laughing. "Master Wisp," he says, "I heard you had a good day."

"I did, sir," Wisp says, and he salutes the colonel. "I played Life with the Dawson boys, and I won."

"Ah, now, then," the colonel says, grinning. "I knew you would soldier on well."

"Are you celebrating something?" Willow's mom asks.

"Oh, just a little bit now, ma'am," the colonel says, "but later tonight, there's a big celebration on the way."

Just then, Old Woman Wallace comes up to their table, a gift wrapped in light blue tissue paper in her hand. Wisp shrinks from her. But when she speaks, her voice is soft and soothing, not like the biting, angry dog she appeared to be earlier, in the kitchen.

Mrs. Wallace rubs her right hand on her apron and then lays the same hand on the colonel's snow-wet arm and hands him the package.

"For her," she says to the colonel. "Congratulations."

The colonel nods. "Much appreciated."

"Give her my love," Mrs. Wallace says.

The colonel nods again.

Something nice is obviously happening. Willow hopes the colonel will fill them in. But instead, he simply salutes the three of them. "Well, I must go check on her now. It will be soon."

He doesn't volunteer any more information, and Willow and her mother are too polite to pry.

Off he marches, leaving the bell on the diner door jangling in his wake.

Willow sleeps through the night and wakes to a day that is swollen with spitting snow, as if God is squeezing out the last of the storm he has sent their way.

At breakfast, Cora is bustling about, dishing out pancakes and bacon and humming a tune. Wisp is wild with excitement over getting to eat these usually forbidden foods. He digs in without a word, worried, Willow is sure, that their mom will stop him before he gets a bite or the illness diminishes his appetite.

But their mom says nothing. She is looking at Cora.

"You seem awfully happy, Cora," Mom says.

The old lady smiles widely. "Yes, I am. Bernadette D'Anjou was rushed to the hospital around midnight last night. She was expecting, but the baby wasn't due for weeks. When she went into labor, it was touch and go for several hours. But around nine this morning, she was successfully delivered of a healthy baby boy. The whole town is just delighted."

"That's wonderful," Mom says. "I'm so glad everything went well."

Cora nods. "Oh, it did. It did. Just as expected. I can't wait to see that little boy."

"Is she still in the hospital?" Mom asks. "Would you like to go with me to see her and the baby? I was going there after breakfast anyway. I'd be happy to help you navigate the snow. With all the slippery conditions, it's a tough walk."

Cora shakes her head, her beaded bracelets clanking a tune. "No need. I'll go when the snow clears. The colonel is there now with her anyway."

"The colonel?" Willow asks before she can stop herself.

"Yes. Bernadette is his granddaughter," Cora tells them.

Willow blinks. Her eyes meet her mom's. They are both clearly remembering the cigars and the blue-wrapped present from Old Woman Wallace, the colonel's happiness and his words of a celebration to come. It is as if the colonel and Mrs. Wallace knew his granddaughter would have a baby this morning. But Cora said Bernadette didn't go into labor until midnight—after the colonel left the diner—and that the child wasn't due for weeks. So how is that possible?

Willow feels a strange sense of unease creep up her back and a tingle run down her spine. She thinks of all the odd things she's seen since arriving in Kismet—Layla and James being on that bridge seconds after the car crash; Cora knowing to put an extra bed and the bucket for Wisp in their room; Cora giving Willow grapefruit juice before Willow said she wanted it; Cora knowing Topher was at the door before he'd knocked; Topher mentioning a secret. And Willow knows in that instant that this little town of Kismet is not what it seems—that something is going on here that is *not* normal.

CHAPTER 11

Willow's mom heads out into the hallway and puts on her coat.

But Willow doesn't want to be left alone in this town where, she is certain, something is not right. Willow can smell the peculiarity of Kismet, like smoke smoldering in a hidden corner, a fire about to ignite. Secrets sizzle here.

She follows her mom to the door. "Are you going to the hospital *now*? You aren't going to leave us by ourselves here *again*, are you?"

But her mom nods. "I won't be long. Keep an eye on Wisp for me."

"Mom?" Willow pleads. "Can't we figure out some way to get home today? This town is weird."

Her mom looks at Willow and sighs. "I agree. There's something strange going on here. Look. They can't hold people back from traveling forever. I'm sure they'll lift the state of emergency in a few hours. And then, yes, I'll find someone to drive us to a car rental place, even if it is miles from here. I want to get home too."

For a moment, Willow feels a connection with her mom that she has not felt in months, a shared concern other than Wisp. And she remembers suddenly how it was when her mom actually worried about her too. She remembers when her mom would tuck her in at night and how her hand would graze Willow's forehead to wake her in the morning; how her mother packed lunches with special messages just for her; how her mother spent time with just her, talking and giggling.

But then her mom puts her hand on the door. "I'll be back soon."

"Mom . . . ," Willow tries again.

Her mom pauses and looks back, and for a second Willow thinks she will stay. But then she turns around again and heads out the door, hurrying through the snow, leaving Willow behind. Willow slowly closes the door on the cold and bites back tears, feeling as if she has just lost a limb. She wants to go home now!

She is about to head back to Wisp in the dining room when the doorbell rings. Willow's heart lifts. Maybe her mom has changed her mind and wants to pack up their things and get out of this creepy little town right away.

But when she opens the door, Topher is standing where her mom should be, his arms full of poles, boots, and skis. Beside him, his two brothers, in coats and mittens and boots, carry even more equipment. "Hey, Willow. Get Wisp, and let's go for a cross-country ski."

"My brother isn't allowed outside," Willow says.

Topher looks her in the eye and Willow's heart misses a beat.

"I bet Wisp will think differently," Topher says. "Besides, as long as you're stuck here, you should do some things." He is inside before Willow can stop him. "Wisp!" he calls. "Come on. We're cross-country skiing up Bain's Hill."

Wisp comes running in his stocking feet. "Okay!"

"You can't go," Willow says, following Topher, exasperation building inside her over this boy who keeps pushing his way into their lives, forcing her to experience odd feelings she doesn't want to feel, hinting at secrets but then refusing to tell her what they are.

"I can too," Wisp argues. "I feel fine right now."

"Wisp, you're not allowed to go outside," Willow says. "You know Mom wouldn't want you to."

"You're not my boss," Wisp says, his voice rising.

"I am when Mom's not here," Willow snaps.

"I want to go!" Wisp yells. "I'm going! I'm going! I'm going!"

"No, you're not," Willow says.

"Yes, I am!" Wisp shouts.

"Enough!" Cora's voice cuts through Wisp's cries as she shuffles her way into the room holding Willow's and Wisp's coats. "Stop yelling in my house. Put your hats and boots on, and take your arguing outside."

Wisp sticks out his tongue at Willow. He is in his coat and out the door before Willow can protest. And what could she have said anyway? Wisp has made it impossible for them to stay inside. Cora has every right to shoo them out.

And now Willow must go along with them. She can't let her brother ski off and get injured. After all, it's an unspoken family rule that Wisp must be careful at all costs.

Willow wishes she were not in charge and the one responsible again, but obviously Wisp has now decided her afternoon for her. So she puts on her coat and boots, hat and mittens, and follows the boys into the snow. As she steps outside the door, Cora puts a hand on Willow's arm.

"Wisp will be all right today," she says, and then, turning quickly, she closes the front door firmly behind her.

Willow stares after her. This is the second time she has said this to Willow. And while she was right yesterday, there is no way she can be one hundred percent positive about how Wisp will fare after a long ski in wet snow and cold weather.

Topher steps near Willow. "Trust her," he says. His breath dances like a snowflake across Willow's face.

"Why?" Willow snaps. "Does she have ESP or something? Or is that a secret too?"

Topher sighs. "Believe me, if Cora says Wisp'll be fine, he will be."

Willow pushes him away, annoyed by this boy who hints at all manner of hidden things but will not answer anything. She skis away fast from him, trying to catch up with Joe Joe, Taddie, and most importantly, Wisp.

Willow calms as she skis along. Reverence is what this world demands, and gratitude is what she gives it.

The world is a white wonderland, and they are its silent inhabitants. Everyone, even Joe Joe and Taddie, is quiet as their skis slice a path through the snow-covered trees near the end of the lake.

Still, without words, it is clear that there is a contest to be won. Each boy pushes hard, trying to outski the others. Even Wisp is moving fast, and Willow worries he will tire long before they finish. She finds herself behind them, not even trying to stay abreast of these boys and join their race for the top, content to just keep Wisp visible.

But at last, they all reach the summit of the hill, frost ballooning from their mouths as they gasp for air. Willow eyes Wisp with concern, but he is fine. His eyes are lit up like two lighthouse beacons.

Suddenly, Willow realizes that she is about to have the fight of her life getting Wisp back before their mom returns and begins a full-blown war should they not be there.

Below them, the town is blanketed in snow, sleepy and serene. As far as the eye can see there is nothing but the little village of Kismet, and the mountains and lake and stone wall that surround it. There isn't another town in sight, not even a billboard or a farm—just Kismet's huddled houses clinging to each other by the south and east sides of the lake, holding one another in a protective embrace. Willow does not know if she has ever been in a place so completely isolated from the rest of the world. They are truly in the middle of nowhere.

Still, it is lovely to look at, and Willow sighs. She does not want to leave, not yet. She wants to stay for just a moment more and enjoy the peace of this snow-whitened world. And so she waits, not wanting to start the nagging process to get her brother home.

"Enjoying the view?" Topher asks.

Willow jumps. She didn't notice he has come to stand beside her.

He gazes out across the valley and toward the hills beyond. "You can see a long way from up here."

"It must be weird living so far from anything," Willow says as she looks out over the distance.

Topher shrugs. "Kismet has its own unique reasons for existing."

"Like what?" Willow smirks. "Its secrets?"

"It's not a big town," Topher says, not really answering, "but it's a close town. Everyone here wants the same kind of life, I guess."

She cannot imagine living in a world without the ability to reach several museums or restaurants. In Burlington, Vermont, where she lives, there are many choices. Here, you'd have next to none.

"Sounds boring," Willow mutters.

Topher laughs slightly. "Well, you're right about that. You're *really* lucky to live somewhere else."

Willow points to the brick building. "What's in there?"

"It's just a hall," Topher says.

"I've watched a few people go in there," Willow says. "What's inside?"

"Nothing you'd want to see," Topher says.

He waves a hand toward the mountains. "Even this boring town has some things that are nice about it. Those mountains are kind of beautiful, right?"

"Yeah, *beautiful*," Willow says, irritated again that he won't answer a simple question.

Her annoyance with him reminds her that she needs to stop fooling around and get Wisp back. Her mom will blame her if he gets sick from being out in the cold.

"It's kind of nice to have someone new in town to hang out with," Topher says, turning and looking into her eyes. "Even if it is only for a couple of days."

He reaches out wool-thick fingers and brushes back a strand of hair that has strayed into her eyes.

At his touch, Willow's stomach flops like a fish pulled from water. She steps back.

"Sorry," Topher says, smiling. "Just thought it was in the way."

Then he nods toward the lake they skied past on their way up the hill. Closer to the center, its icy top is covered with thick snow, but at the near end, the surface shines like newly polished stone.

"That's where we skate," he tells her. "The town keeps it clear and checks the ice to be sure it's solid. Want to go skating tonight? I mean, since you're still here. They light up the lake. It'll be fun."

"Fun" is a word that dropped out of Willow's vocabulary two years ago. School, homework, the laundry her mother forgot to do, the dirty dishes in the sink, the house that's been left a mess, doctor visits with Wisp—this has been Willow's world recently. There has been no room for lights, music, and laughter. And they *are* leaving Kismet, hopefully in a few hours—tomorrow at the latest. There is no point in letting this boy wiggle his way into her life.

But before Willow can answer, a snowball hits Topher square in the back. Wisp, Joe Joe, and Taddie have taken off their skis, fallen to their knees, and made a snowball fort. A battle has begun with snowball ammunition, and suddenly, Topher and Willow are warding off an attack. Their enemy laughs and giggles as they pelt Topher and Willow.

Topher's eyes flash with delight as he whips off his skis too. "Come on, Willow. Charge!"

And for an instant, Willow's sadness lifts a little, and she takes off her skis and follows his lead, running toward the boys. They fall on top of them, grabbing their heads and stuffing them in the snow. The boys fight hard, shoving snow down Topher's and Willow's backs. They all howl and holler.

"Snow angel time!" Willow shouts.

They all fall on their backs and wave their arms around,

making wings in the white powder. Then they stand and look at the perfect circle of angels they've made.

But then Joe Joe throws another snowball, and soon they are all pummeling each other again. They dash and dodge, bombarding one another and laughing loudly.

Finally, they are exhausted. They all fall down and lie quietly on their backs in the snow and the silence, and for the first time in a long time, Willow feels a smile on her lips—until she notices that the sun has begun to sink in the sky and the shadows of an early-winter afternoon are beginning to creep in.

Willow jumps to her feet, her heart thumping. Her mom is going to be furious that Wisp is not safely resting inside, and Willow will be the one to blame. "We have to get back."

She pulls Wisp to his feet, and the others rise reluctantly. Soon they are off, heading down the hill. But this time, Willow is in front, leading the charge.

She has screwed up. She has let Wisp out and let him run wild. It is so unlike her. She is Wisp's reliable sister. A surge of guilt runs through her for breaking the family rules.

"Hurry!" Willow urges them all, and the boys move faster, though Wisp falls behind a bit as his energy wanes.

At last, they come to Cora's house. Willow's heart stops when she sees the front door open and their mom standing there.

But surprisingly, her mom doesn't look worried. Her brows are not raised in fury, as Willow expected. Instead, her mom is smiling, as though they have won some great prize.

"Did you have fun?" she asks as Wisp curls about her legs and Willow begins stumbling for an explanation.

"Come inside," Mom says. "I have some news."

Willow's stomach sinks to her booted feet. She does not need to ask.

Her mom has found a new test or treatment for Wisp. Already, Willow can feel the happiness of this afternoon floating away like a snowflake swirled skyward by the wind. She shakes snow from her hat and helps Wisp take off his boots and mittens and coat. They wait together to hear what their mom has to say.

She smiles at them both and says the thing that Willow was afraid might be coming: "I think we may stay in Kismet for a while."

CHAPTER 12

Willow blinks. What did her mother say?

A quick test, a day or two of treatment, Willow could understand. But stay here for *a while*? What does that mean? Willow is as blown away by her mother's words as the snowflakes on Cora's windows are by the whipping wind.

"You're talking about until the roads are cleared, right?" Willow manages to finally ask.

Their mom shakes her head. "No," she says, continuing slowly. "I'm thinking we'll stay on a little longer than that. I may even rent a house when this storm is over. I have a few more things to check out. I've talked to some people, and I think it would be helpful for Wisp to be here."

"Yippee!" Wisp yells. He runs about the room like a crazed squirrel, high-fiving anything in his path: a wall, a chair, a door.

"Why?" Willow asks—the real question that needs an answer.

"There's a wonderful hospital here," Mom says, lowering her voice so Wisp will not hear. "I met those boys' mother, and we talked. She's got some ideas for Wisp—and for us. I think we should give them a try."

So, a treatment has been suggested, and once again, all arguments fall away in the face of Wisp's illness. And who is Willow to disagree? Wisp *has* to come first. Her wants and needs are hardly as important. After all, she is the healthy child.

But it must be a long treatment or many tests if her mom is willing to consider renting a place. And then Willow thinks of *him*.

"But Dad—" Willow says before she can stop herself.

Her mom's face tightens, but before she can say anything, Cora comes into the dining room, carrying a plate of food.

"Cookies?" Cora asks.

Wisp runs to her side. He reaches for a treat before their mom can protest.

The smell filling the room is pure chocolate chip, and Willow would be almost weak with wanting a cookie after her exertions this day if she weren't so consumed with the ridiculous decision her mother is considering.

"I like it here," Wisp says between bites as he devours the treat he has shoved into his mouth.

"Of course you like it here," Willow snaps. "But what about home? What about our friends?"

She sees Wisp frown and immediately regrets her words.

Friends. Wisp has none anymore. Eight-year-olds do not want to hang out with other eight-year-olds who cannot run around or eat french fries. Over time, all of Wisp's friends have drifted away, like survivors from a sinking vessel. Only Wisp has been left to captain on, alone.

But then she remembers her own friends. She thinks of Elise and her teammates, her school and her teachers—all the things in her life that have been her rocks during this unhappy upheaval. What about *her* friends? For two years, Willow has been living a held-hostage kind of life, her every move dictated by Wisp's needs. Now this?

"Not forever," Willow says, turning back to her mom. "Just a week or so, right? At the most a month?"

Her mom pauses, and her eyes flick to the left. Willow catches her breath.

Did her mom just exchange a glance with Cora? Why would Cora have anything to do with this decision? Uneasiness snakes its way into Willow's heart.

"Mom!" she says, trying to redirect her mother's attention, to make her focus on Willow, on *them,* not Cora. "Not forever, right?"

Her mom smiles in that way that always makes Willow's insides heat with anger, as if Willow is acting like a baby. "It's far too early to decide something like that," her mom says. "We'll have to wait and see how Wisp's treatments go, if I decide to try them."

"What treatments?" Wisp says, all ears now that he is no longer hungry. Chocolate decorates the side of his lips.

"Just a few little things I'd like to try, Wisp," Mom says. She brushes the hair out of his eyes, licks her thumb, and scrubs away the chocolate from his face. "And no more cookies, please. You know those aren't good for you."

"Milk and cookies are always good for the soul," Cora says.

She gives Willow's mom a long look, and Willow sees her mother nod. What is going on here? What has Cora done to her mom? Who is Cora to decide a DuChard future?

"I don't want any more treatments," Wisp says, his mouth twisting up in a scowl worthy of the Grinch.

"I know you don't, sweetie," Mom says. "But it won't be bad. I promise."

DuChard *Spoken* Family Rule #3: Always be patient with the patient.

"I don't want to," Wisp repeats.

"Well, it's not something you have to worry about now, okay?" Mom says in a calm voice.

"Another cookie?" Cora asks, holding out the plate to Wisp.

Cora has won the day and distracted him. Wisp's hand rises wearily to take his second prize away.

"Cookie?" Cora asks Willow, extending the plate.

Willow ignores her, refusing to be that easily bribed or swayed. Bubbling, simmering anger oozes through her.

"This is stupid," she says.

"We'll talk about it more later, Willow. I haven't even made a definite decision yet. I'm still thinking on it. No reason to get upset," Mom says, and she turns away so the discussion can't go on without making everyone uncomfortable. It's one of her favorite strategies in the midst of a battle—the distraction, the delay tactic. But Willow has a few tricks of her own. She is not about to surrender.

She sneaks into Cora's kitchen and finds the only phone in town. Before her mom can start looking for her, Willow dials her dad's number.

When he answers, relief loosens the knot that has lodged itself in her gut. Willow is giddy with the promise of salvation.

"Dad," she says, and her voice is earthshakingly unsteady. "Dad."

"I'm here, Willow," her dad says.

"Mom's lost it again," Willow says. "She's heard about some new treatment, and she's saying we may stay here in Kismet for a while."

There is a long pause on the other end of the line, and suddenly, Willow feels as if her insides have just blown up in one long, terrible explosion.

Her mom already told him.

"Dad, I have school," Willow reminds him, panic gripping her hard, "and hockey."

He sighs. "Hockey's over for Christmas break, Willow. And I'm sure your mom is only considering a week or so."

His voice holds the hope of a fool searching for paradise.

He is grasping onto the belief that Willow's mom will give up eventually and come home.

But Willow knows better. If there is a sliver of a chance of curing Wisp or even just figuring out what he actually has, Willow will have new classmates in Maine come January 3. She can't believe this is happening to her. She longs for adulthood and the ability to walk away from this foolishness. But she's only twelve, and so she's stuck.

"I miss you, Willow," Dad says, his voice low with longing.

THEN DO SOMETHING! Willow wants to scream at him in surround sound. *GET UP HERE!* But her mouth stays shut.

"We'll talk every day, okay, Willow?" Dad says.

"Sure," Willow says. She hangs up the phone without saying goodbye, the only rebellion she can eke out of this situation that stinks stronger than sweaty hockey equipment.

Tears trickle down her face, and then she is surprised to find a tissue thrust at her.

"It would be nice to know what will happen, wouldn't it?" Cora says. "To be better prepared when hard times come your way?"

Willow does not want comfort right now. She wants to be alone. She wants to be at home. She wants to be with her friends. She wants to talk to Elise. She wants Wisp to get better. She wants Mom to stop obsessing. She wants Dad to take charge and do something for once. She wants to hit something. She wants her stuff back from the river. She wants her hockey stick so she can whack a puck so hard it shatters glass. She wants. She wants. She wants.

But Willow knows that her wants are relegated to the back row in the theater of their lives, and Wisp must take center stage.

So she says nothing. She swallows her anger and turns her head and walks away. It is what she is best at these days.

Dinner at the diner is awkward. Wisp is tired, and his stomach is rebelling. He picks at his food, moving it from side to side but eating nothing. Still, he manages to smile as he talks about staying in this town, obviously enjoying being able to eat what he likes, run wild outside, and make new friends. Willow feels like Scrooge, still wanting to go home and take all that away from him.

Fewer people are out tonight, and Old Woman Wallace is noticeably absent from her place in the kitchen. For a moment, Willow wonders again how the restaurant owner had a gift wrapped up to give the colonel before the baby was even born. *Maybe,* Willow thinks, *the woman just gives presents ahead of time.*

When they are done eating, Mom and Willow make their way back to Cora's in the early-evening darkness with Wisp draped like a coat in their mother's arms, exhausted. The night has cleared, and stars sprinkle the sky. Just Willow's luck that their mom made her discovery earlier today, or, no doubt, they would be homeward bound first thing tomorrow morning.

Willow thinks about her teammates again. They're probably all texting now and making plans for the rest of the winter vacation. If she is to stay here for longer than a week, her mother *must* get her a new cell phone and let her call Elise. It is the least she can do.

At Cora's, Willow goes straight to their room and throws on the pajamas Layla brought them.

"Sweet dreams," Cora calls after her, but Willow doesn't answer. Instead, she curls into a self-righteous ball of cold anger on the bed. Suddenly, she hears the doorbell ring.

"Willow?" Cora calls from the stairs in her rich, raspy voice. "Topher is here."

CHAPTER 13

Topher? And then she remembers his idea to go skating tonight.

There's a part of her that wants to say she can't go. After all, he's the one who told her mom about his doctor mother. He is the very reason she is stuck here tonight, like a beetle thrown on its back that can do nothing but wave its legs helplessly in the air.

But another part of her wants to pay him back for his interfering in her life. The idea is oddly appealing—certainly more enticing than sitting by herself, all angry and frustrated.

So she gets up and scurries around the room, grabbing her clothes from the chair, shoving legs, arms, head through the appropriate holes. Her mom has washed their clothes each night in the B&B's laundry room, but Willow has been in the same jeans and shirt since she arrived in Kismet. She wonders if it is obvious.

She quickly tugs a brush through her hair and goes downstairs, knowing she probably looks a wreck. But Topher doesn't even seem to notice. He holds up a pair of hockey skates. "I think Joe Joe's will fit you. Are you ready to go?"

"Sure," Willow says. "I'm ready."

And she is. After all, he doesn't know how well she can skate. She plans to run rings around him on the ice.

When they get to the lake, the lights are on, and a lot of kids have already laced up. They glide in slow circles around the area that has been scraped clean and watered down to create a smooth, clear surface. Across from the skating area stands the large brick building Willow saw people going in and out of—a "hall," as Topher said.

Music plays from speakers set high in the trees. The songs are slow and syrupy. If Willow were home and getting ready to take to the ice, her music would have a roaring, rushing, pounding beat that would be meant to get her and Elise and her teammates all hyped up to shove and push and fight for that little black puck. Willow is glad that is not what she is hearing now. She isn't sure she would be able to hold it together if a song were playing that reminded her that she is here while Elise is basking in the sun on vacation and her other friends are where she longs to be—back home in Burlington. Willow sits down on a bench beside Topher and slides her shoes off.

"You skate much?" he asks.

Willow lies. "A little."

She feels bad about lying, but what will happen if they stay past the beginning of the year? Will she be forced to deal with a new school and friends? Angrily, she starts to lace up her skates, pulling them tightly; then she sees Topher eyeing her curiously. Willow looks like a pro at this, which is what she is. Immediately, she drops the laces.

"Do you need some help?" Topher asks, standing.

Willow nods. She holds out the laces.

She can't wait to see his face when she finally skates circles around him.

He kneels down in front of her like a knight about to swear fealty. Seeing him like this stops Willow for a moment. He looks up, and Willow sees his flushed cheeks and his easy smile and her heart thumps—two long slow beats. He takes the laces from her hands and quickly has her skates tied up tightly. His fingers graze her bare calf when he tries to pull the leg of her jeans back down over the skate. The surprise of his touch zings her deep in the gut.

Topher's face goes red. He laughs slightly and stands up. Then he sits again to put on his own skates.

Willow has to admit—he has nice blades, the new and expensive kind where you can mold the skate to the contour of your foot by heating up an inner layer. Willow's goalie skates fit her the same way. Or at least, they *did* fit her the same way. Now the skates that were a Christmas present from her dad are sliding across rocks and sandy river bottoms toward the sea. Their loss reminds Willow again that she is not here for fun.

She may be stuck here because of this boy. She must ignore her heart and belly.

Topher stands. "Come on. I'll help you onto the ice."

Willow hesitates, trying to look newbie afraid.

"Don't be scared," Topher says, grinning. "I won't let you go."

Willow takes his hand. His fingers are smooth and warm. He grips her fingers tightly, and she gets to her feet. He pulls her to him, closer than she expected.

His eyes meet hers and then slide down to her lips. And suddenly, Willow has to remind herself to breathe, breathe, breathe, for she seems to have forgotten how to do this seemingly ordinary task. What is wrong with her?

There is a sudden swish of blades.

"Hey, Topher."

Willow turns her head. Two girls about her age are standing near them on the icy lake.

"What do you want?" Topher asks, and his tone is not friendly.

"Hi," one of the girls says, not answering him but instead turning to Willow. Her hair beneath her hat is as red as her cheeks, her skin as white as her perfect teeth. "I'm Angeline. I heard you might be moving here."

Beside her, Willow senses Topher stiffening. He drops her hand.

And Willow wonders, *Does everyone in this town know everybody else's business?*

Then she remembers that is why Topher's father left. For a moment, she feels a sudden kinship with this man she's never met.

"I doubt it," Willow says, wanting to hold on to the small sliver of hope that her mom will come to her senses. After all, she said she hadn't decided yet.

"This is Grace," Angeline says, nodding toward the other girl, whose dark hair and skin jump into sharp relief against the snowy ground. Her eyelids are smudged dark green, her lips bright red.

"Come on," Angeline says. "We'll help you." She holds out her hand for Willow, but there is no helpfulness in the girl's expression.

Before Willow can refuse, Angeline takes Willow's hand and jerks her hard onto the ice. Willow nearly stumbles with the force of the pull.

Angeline puts her lips near Willow's ear. Her breath slides across Willow's cheek, light and smooth like falling feathers.

"I know you can skate," Angeline whispers. "Don't think pretending will work with him."

Willow's head snaps around, and she meets Angeline's eyes. She winks at Willow, and Willow shivers.

"How do you know that?" she can't help but ask.

Angeline grins. "Oh, that's my secret, for now. But maybe soon it will be yours too. Wouldn't that be fun?"

"What?" Willow says, staring into Angeline's eyes.

"It's all up to your mother now," Angeline says, soft and low.

Willow sways without meaning to, more unsettled than unstable. What does this girl mean?

Angeline grins and pushes Willow away. Topher is quickly at Willow's side, his hand sliding back into hers.

"I've got you," he says to Willow.

"Keep an eye on her, Topher," Angeline says, laughing. "And don't say we didn't warn you."

Grace grins too before they both skate off, leaving Topher and Willow alone again.

Willow's mind is reeling with what Angeline has said—the strange fact that somehow Angeline knew she could skate even though they've never met, and that somehow her mom has something to do with Angeline being aware of this.

"Are you guys friends?" Willow manages to ask as the girls move farther away from them.

Topher shrugs. "Sometimes. They're both a year ahead of me and are always reminding me that they know more than I do." He rolls his eyes and tugs on her hand. "Come on. Let's skate."

Topher pulls her into the circle, and Willow's thoughts are brought abruptly back to the reason she is here tonight—how she wanted to knock this boy off his pedestal of confidence.

So who cares what that girl said? Who cares if she knows that Willow can skate? Really, who cares what any of them say? They are all odd, and she'll never be friends with them anyway.

She has come out tonight to show Topher up, and that is what she is going to do.

She and Topher join the other skaters in their slow promenade.

Around and around they go. And Willow wonders, not for the first time, why public skating is always like this—skaters moving in slow circles, always in one direction. There's never a dart across the wide empty middle, never a sudden push or shove. It is predictable, controlled, dull as dirty laundry. It is all Willow can do not to yawn as they slide in this mind-numbing pattern—that is, until she spies a hockey game in progress at the other side of the lake, near the brick building.

Willow can stand these repetitive, plodding movements no longer. She wants to fly, to spin, to break this endless circling, to be part of that game. It's time to show Topher what she can do.

She drops his hand and pushes away. And then she is off, racing toward the far end of the lake, splitting that sleep-inducing skaters' circle in half, dodging around kids, whizzing past couples, jumping over sneakers left haphazardly at the edge of the ice, her skates flying, her heart soaring. She is good at this. She is great at this. She is the best there is at this.

She has flown to within fifty yards of the hockey game when she hears Topher calling to her.

"Willow, watch out!"

And suddenly, before her is a broken patch of ice, like a

mouth open wide and waiting. And in that moment, Willow feels fear force itself up from her gut. She is a great skater, but as a goalie, she is not a swift stopper. Willow turns her blades outward, trying desperately to stop or slow. But she does not know if she will make it, or if in a minute more, she will be hurtled feetfirst into the icy waters of a lake in Kismet, Maine.

CHAPTER 14

In a whirlwind of motion, Willow is gripped from behind. With a quickness and strength that takes her breath away, Topher pulls her back just inches before she hits the rim of the large hole in the ice.

When they are out of danger, Topher throws back his head and lets out a belly laugh so filled with delight that it tingles deep inside Willow.

Willow is not a clumsy girl given to death-defying stunts, so she cannot catch her breath, let alone laugh like Topher. If it hadn't been for him, she would have plunged into icy waters cold enough to whip away all thoughts, all breath, all life. Fear twirls thin, cold strands of rope around her throat, squeezing hard. She begins to shake uncontrollably.

Topher stops laughing and puts a hand on her shoulder, trying to steady her. "Hey. It's okay. You're all right."

Before Willow can protest or even think about what's happening, Topher pulls her close and holds her tight against him.

Now her head begins to spin, her mind boomeranging from

her near-death experience to this warm hug. She cannot fight them both, so she lets him hold her. She sinks into the warmth of him until her breathing slows.

At last, he releases her and steps back.

He blushes. "I just . . . I just wanted to make sure you were all right. You seemed really scared."

"I'm okay," Willow lies.

Topher's eyes twinkle. "I didn't expect you to be able to skate like that."

It's what she wanted him to say. But instead, she's the one wobbling with uncertainty, not Topher. Her confusion whooshes away, and anger surges in.

"Why is there nothing on the ice to warn people about that open water?" she snaps. "Any other lake or pond open to public skating by the town would have warning signs and tape or those bright orange cones to stop people from coming near it."

Topher shrugs, all innocent. "I guess 'cause people from here know about it. It's my fault. I should have told you. But I didn't expect you to take off like that. There's a hot spring under the lake that keeps this end unfrozen. It's been like that forever." He nods toward the brick building. "That thing was built as a protection for the thermal spring. The open hole is where the warm water rushes out and meets the cold waters of the lake."

He smiles. "Some say the waters are magical."

His eyes wander down to her lips again, and Willow feels her heart beat, beat.

She makes herself step away. She needs to think. She needs air.

Coming close to danger like that plays games with your head.

Willow thinks of Wisp and all his gory thoughts. And she believes she understands him better now. He is looking for something to grab onto in his uncertain world, as a man overboard will thrash for a life preserver. He wants to understand the risk he lives with.

"Where were you headed?" Topher asks, an amused smile playing on his lips.

Willow swallows, avoiding his eyes, steeling herself not to betray her confused feelings. She points toward the other side of the ice. "I thought I'd join the game."

"You play hockey?"

Willow nods.

"Great," he says. "Let's do it, then. Are you good to go?"

Willow nods again. Yes, she wants to play. Unlike her brother, she longs to leave this unsettling experience behind as quickly as she can. She does not want to examine it or think about these disturbing moments. Willow wants to ignore it all.

When they get to the game, the kids there are more than happy to have a real goalie. Willow is soon in the equipment of a boy who happens to be her size, even though he's younger than she is.

Willow is put on one team as goalie. Topher joins the other team as a forward. The thought of thrashing around in icy-cold water is quickly replaced by slap shots, breakaways, sweat, goals, and saves. Willow's regular breathing returns, and her familiar and reassuring defensive skills take over.

Her new team members are swift and determined. The game moves up and down the ice. Finally, one boy on Willow's team zooms by their opponents. He shoots and scores.

But a moment later, she sees Topher heading toward her on a breakaway, bearing straight down on her, playing the puck close to his body. As he skates hard toward her, Willow moves out from the net, ready to stop him if she has to. He suddenly shoots. And Willow dives to block his shot, but she misses. The puck slides into the net just as Topher crashes into Willow, and together, they tumble, sliding hard in a tangle of net and skates and sticks.

Topher is laughing that deep laugh that tickles and tingles inside Willow and sets her to laughing too. And once again, as on the hilltop, Willow is, in that moment, happy. Happy again.

And it is such a relief to remember happiness, to let it in, to let it fill her up, that Willow decides she must forgive Topher. She has no choice. Because she realizes that she likes him. Willow likes Topher Dawson.

He walks her back to Cora's. The snow has stopped, and stars fill the sky. Willow hasn't felt this free in two years. The monster that's been sitting on her chest for months seems to have temporarily gone off to haunt someone else.

The lake waters of Kismet, Maine, may or may not be magical, but this night has been filled with magic for her.

At Cora's door, Willow leans back against the wood of the inn and breathes in the night, wishing she could hold it inside her for always. Topher smiles at her.

"You're really good," he says.

"Thanks," Willow says. "You're good too."

He laughs. "Well, everyone in Kismet is practically born on skates. Winters are too long here not to learn."

"I had fun tonight."

Topher nods, serious now. "I did too." He mismatch stares at her. "You . . ."

He pauses, looks away for a moment, then swings his eyes back to her. "You surprise me. I like that. I like spontaneity, unpredictability. Don't you?"

His question seems odd. Who doesn't like surprises?

"Of course," Willow says.

He hesitates and Willow wonders if he will finally reveal the secret he keeps alluding to.

Finally, he looks up at her with those eyes of his. "Thanks for one of the best days ever, Willow," he whispers.

If Willow could hit pause on some movie of her life, she would do it now so she could always replay this very moment.

He sighs. "If only . . ."

"If only what?" Willow asks, surprised that there is an "if only."

Topher laughs and shrugs. "Nothing. Forget it."

She wishes she knew why it always seems like he is keeping something from her, and she is tempted to press him for an answer. But she also doesn't want to ruin this night.

And soon, the moment for asking has passed, for Topher says, "See you tomorrow?"

Willow nods. "Sure."

Topher grins and jumps from the porch, giving her a wave. "Sweet dreams," he calls over his shoulder.

He walks down the hill from Cora's toward town. Like a fragment of a thought, he is soon swallowed in darkness, appearing and reappearing each time he passes the streetlights that wind their way toward the center of town, and Willow is alone on Cora's porch with a smile still on her face.

She cannot go to sleep. Her mind reruns her own personal You-Tube of skate and scare, of hug and game and hug again. She is only able to drift off long after she hears the clock in Cora's living room chiming the midnight hour.

So she is surprised to wake in the very early morning, and even more surprised to find that her mom is not beside her. The bathroom is dark. The only sound she hears is Wisp turning in his sleep.

Willow waits. But her mom does not come back.

Unable to resist her curiosity any longer, Willow climbs

from the warm bed and makes her way to the window. In the moonlight of an after-storm sky, Willow can see clearly down to the brick building by the lake. And there is Cora, plain as day, working her way toward the building. Then Willow's breathing halts, because there too is her mother.

CHAPTER 15

Willow runs to put on her clothes. She wants to find out what is in that building that would explain why her mother is wandering outside with Cora in the middle of the night. Could it have something to do with what Angeline said? But suddenly, with the sound of a small beeper, Willow realizes that Wisp's nausea drug must be wearing off.

Normally their mom wakes up in the middle of the night to give Wisp his medicine. She never forgets. But Willow sees that Wisp's pill is still sitting next to his bed. How could her mother leave before Wisp took his medication?

Willow wants to follow her mom, but she has no choice. She has to stay.

She shakes Wisp gently, and he wakes up unfazed. One small pill, one small sip of water and sleep pulls him down again.

Willow stands, unable to move from his side. She watches as Wisp's eyes flutter with dreams. And she remembers those days when they were younger, when he was always trying to keep up with her, and how she sometimes pushed him away. He was the annoying baby brother, the kid in the way, someone to pick on and tease, someone to leave behind when Willow went on her adventures with Elise hiking through the woods, skating on ponds, bike riding the streets.

His lashes lie lightly against the dark circles under his eyes. His thin body gives a slight shake.

What if he does die? She knows she isn't supposed to let her mind go there, but she can't forget her father telling her mother that the doctors said it was a possibility.

Willow thinks of all the things about Wisp that she would miss if that awful thing should happen: the way his voice is always at shouting pitch inside or out; how he runs through their house at warp Wisp speed, knocking things over and never stopping; how his grubby hands are always on her things, marking them like an animal marks his territory. She has to admit—she would miss his bad-mannered boyishness.

And Willow knows in that moment too why she doesn't tell Wisp she loves him. If she says I love you to Wisp, which she rarely does, she will change her relationship with him, because she would only be saying it in case he should die. So is she really any different from her mom, who keeps on fighting? Willow too wills her brother's body to try harder to heal.

But maybe, she thinks, *loving someone who is ill means finding the courage to face the pain you know will be yours if the unthinkable should happen.* Maybe she and her mother are not saviors and battlers and solid rocks but selfish, flawed humans who do not want to suffer.

Willow moves nearer to her brother's bed. She takes a deep breath, steadies herself as she does when faced with the threat of the puck coming near her net. And she wills herself to have courage and take a baby step while he is sleeping, when no one will hear but the night. She bends over him.

"I love you, Wisp," she whispers.

Softly, he whispers back. "I love you too, Willow," and Willow jumps in surprise.

"Fooled ya," he says, grinning. "You thought I was asleep. Ha!"

Willow grins back, and then they both laugh out loud.

Willow will not leave her brother alone tonight. She can ask her mom what she was doing up in the middle of the night tomorrow.

Instead, she pulls the quilt off her bed and slips into a chair near her brother. And she sits and rocks until at last, she hears her brother's steady sleeping breath. Then she closes her eyes and relaxes into sleep too.

When Willow wakes, she is back in the bed she shares with her mom, and her mom is asleep next to her. Sunshine is streaming in through the bedroom windows, heightened and brightened by the white world it shines down on.

Her mom stirs, and Willow waits. Finally, her mom opens her eyes, and when she does, she surprises Willow by smiling.

"Good morning," she says, reaching out a hand to stroke Willow's hair. "You must be feeling great. You slept so deeply last night."

"Did you notice this when you finally came back from *leaving* us?" Willow asks.

But her mom just laughs. "Oh, you did sleep deeply. I didn't leave last night. You must have been dreaming."

Her maniacal happiness is haunting, but her lying is even scarier.

"That's not true," Willow protests. "I got up and gave Wisp his medicine. You weren't here."

Willow looks over to where Wisp is sleeping, for backup. But his bed is empty.

"Willow, you were dreaming, that's all," Mom says, her voice soothing, reassuring. "No need to worry. Not anymore."

But worrying is all her mom knows these days. It is what defines her. Willow stares at her in confusion.

Her mom pushes back the covers and bounces out of bed. "I'm starving."

She pulls on her clothes, runs a brush quickly through her hair. "Let's go eat, and then we should see about buying some new clothes. A replacement credit card will be arriving today."

She is out of the room before Willow can protest.

A scream of frustration bubbles into Willow's throat. Biting it back, as she usually does these days, she makes herself think of how camels can go seven days without food or water, even in the driest of climates. She can be patient too.

But then she is hit with doubt and her mind burns with questions. Was she dreaming? And if she was, why the same dream with Cora? Why the same brick building? And what did Angeline mean when she said it was up to her mother to reveal Angeline's secret? Does this have to do with the secret Topher has too?

Willow finally gets out of bed and brushes her teeth. She stares at herself in the mirror and concentrates on the two most important questions right now: Is she losing her mind? Or is her mother really lying to her?

Willow throws on her clothes and heads to the dining room, determined to grill Wisp. He will remember.

But Wisp is nowhere to be found. Neither is her mother. Instead, at the table eating french toast are Topher's brothers, Taddie and Joe Joe.

Willow stops, startled.

"Hey, Willow," Taddie says, grinning. "Do you always sleep this late?"

"Where's Wisp?" Willow asks. "Where's my mom?"

"They just left to go see my mom," Joe Joe says.

"We're here to plan Topher's birthday," Taddie says, his feet swinging Wisplike back and forth under the table. "You want to help, don't you? Topher's working at the diner this morning, so we can start decorating and he won't even know anything about it."

"Help with what?" Willow asks.

Taddie rolls his eyes, but Joe Joe elbows him in the gut.

"Topher is going to be thirteen in two days. Remember?" Taddie says. "We're getting his party ready. Do you want to help or not?"

Cora comes in then, plopping down a plate. "Eat up, Willow. Your mom said you're to go lend the boys and some of the other kids in town a hand decorating."

"But . . . ," Willow says, still baffled and bewildered. She feels like a piece of Play-Doh being poked and prodded into a shape some sculptor has predetermined.

"Turning thirteen is a big deal in Kismet," Cora says. "The whole town celebrates. It will be good for you to go with the boys. You can meet other kids your age."

Willow met plenty of kids yesterday during the hockey game. She wants to say no and go find her mother.

But her mom would not welcome her disobeying, turning up at the hospital for a confrontation in front of Wisp's doctor. Willow has no choice right now. She must do as her mother has asked. So she sits and eats her breakfast, and when everyone is finished, she puts on her coat and hat and mittens and boots and follows Taddie and Joe Joe out into a blindingly beautiful winter day.

Without protest, Willow walks duckling-like after them down the road, until the boys begin to run and she sees where they are headed.

The brick building.

CHAPTER 16

Willow follows the boys up the stairs to the mysterious building. Maybe now she will find her answers—find out why Cora and her mother left their warm beds at four o'clock in the morning, and why so many other people wander inside during the day. Willow is almost certain that the secret Topher and Angeline keep alluding to is somehow tied to this building. After all, something in here drew her mother out late last night.

But if Willow expected a chamber of horrors or some other shocking sight, she is to be disappointed. She steps into nothing more than a boring old cavernlike town hall—just as Topher said—with marked-up walls, folding chairs, a stage, and fluorescent lights. There are about twenty kids there, hanging crepe paper and signs and setting up tables. And there are two men and a woman sawing away on fiddles, pausing a few times to discuss something and then starting again, their practice session livening up an already buzzing hive of a place.

Willow looks around, her thoughts tumbling in confusion. There is nothing here. Nothing. Nothing at all.

Maybe she *is* crazy. Why on earth would her mom leave them to come here—to this nothingness?

Willow is one-hundred-piece puzzled. But deep in her gut, she feels she is missing something.

Across the room, Angeline waves to Willow and walks over, her dark shadow, Grace, treading doggedly in her footsteps.

"Hey, Willow," Angeline says. "I knew you'd come right at this very minute."

Willow stares at Angeline. Once again, Angeline has suggested that she already knows what Willow will do and exactly when she will do it.

"How?" Willow asks, realizing she sounds rude.

"What?" Angeline asks, smiling.

"How did you know I'd come right now?" Willow barks.

Angeline laughs and shrugs and winks at Willow. "Guess I'm just psychic." Then she holds up a long sheet of paper. "We were just going to hang this sign. Want to help? Grace and I can hold the ends, and you can let us know if it's straight."

Willow glances distractedly at the banner and blinks at the message written there.

HAPPY 13TH BIRTHDAY, TOPHER.
WELCOME TO KISMET.

"Welcome to Kismet?" Willow says. "But Topher already lives here."

Angeline smiles. "Of course he does. This would look great right here, don't you think?"

She holds the sign up and Grace holds the other end. Neither of them will meet Willow's eyes.

"I need a chair. Can you get me one?" Angeline asks.

Though Angeline has obviously heard Willow, she doesn't offer any explanation as to what the sign means.

Willow shakes her head in irritation. She can't keep being impolite, pushy with tons of questions. Still, she stands there, her anger growing. Why will no one in this town give her answers?

She wants to know what is going on but can't see how to figure it out when people keep ignoring her. So she does as Angeline asks and gets a chair, thinking hard as she drags it across the wooden floor and then goes to get another for Grace.

The girls climb up and hold the sign, then look to Willow for approval, though why they care what Willow thinks is another dumb mystery.

Willow nods that the banner is straight, and they attach it to the wall with tape.

Not far from her, Willow sees Taddie filling a balloon with helium. Then she sees that Wisp is with him. He has come in with their mom, who is standing and talking to a lady with jet-black and slightly gray hair twisted in a long braid that hangs down her back. The woman is reed thin and dressed in hospital scrubs. Willow gazes at her curiously, realizing she must be Topher's mother.

She hears a giggle and looks over to where Wisp and Taddie are standing together. Wisp glances back at their mom, making sure she is not watching, and he takes a breath of the helium. When Joe Joe comes to help, Wisp says, "Hello, Joe Joe," in a helium-induced Munchkin-like voice. Taddie collapses to the floor in a fit of laughter. Willow cannot help herself. She too laughs at Wisp's high jinks.

"Your brother seems to like it here just fine."

Willow turns. Dark-haired, scowling Grace has spoken at last.

"Yeah," Willow says. "He likes Topher's brothers."

"What's your problem, then?" Grace asks, her mouth twitching like the tail of an unhappy cat. "It's obvious you want to get out of Kismet."

"No problem," Willow says, surprised by Grace's rudeness. "I'd just rather be with my own friends back in my own home."

Grace's dark, shadowed eyes glint. "Well, I wish you were back there too."

"Grace," Angeline snaps, coming up beside them.

Grace jumps. And though Angeline may believe that Willow hasn't seen, Willow has. Angeline has just given her friend a wicked pinch on the thin skin of her underarm. Now Angeline reaches out to take hold of Willow. Willow flinches. But Angeline links her arm with Willow's anyway, as if they have been friends since kindergarten. Firmly, she pulls Willow away from Grace.

"She doesn't like strangers," Angeline whispers to Willow

in a conspiratorial voice once they are out of earshot. "Her family has lived here for generations. They were one of the first families of Kismet. She's kind of prickly about new families moving in."

Who would move here, Willow wonders, *to this middle of nowhere—to this nothingness? And why?* Other than her mother's desperate search for Wisp's miracle cure, Willow can't imagine a reason anyone would *choose* to live in this strange place.

"Do new families move here very often?" Willow asks, pulling her arm out of pinching distance from Angeline's pointed and painted nails now that they have made it to the far side of the room. Angeline's creepy friendliness is freaking Willow out.

"No, not many," Angeline says. "But some. My parents are always telling me that there is no place on earth like it."

"Why?" Willow asks.

Angeline shrugs. "I don't know. I've never been anywhere else."

Willow stares. "Never? As in, you've never left Kismet?"

Angeline smiles. "No. Why would I?"

"You've never gone on a vacation or played a sport at another school or driven to Portland or something?" Willow asks.

"No," Angeline says. "None of us have."

Grace comes to stand beside Angeline. "We don't leave," the serious, ill-tempered girl says, looking Willow full in the face, challenging, defiant.

"Why not?" Willow asks, her voice edged with amazement. Anticipation shimmies down her spine. Perhaps this is the secret—the reason no one leaves Kismet. Maybe she'll get some answers rather than feeling pulled in and then pushed away.

But once again, the girls ignore Willow.

Angeline says, "Layla's here with the table decorations."

Willow turns to see Layla struggling into the building, holding a large box, her arms draped in navy cloth.

"Hey, y'all." Layla's voice rings out in the cavelike space, soaring above the musicians, who are now tapping their feet to some Acadian rhythm. "I've brought the tablecloths and napkins and the name cards." She pauses. "I could use some help."

The little kids run to her side, and Angeline and Grace move away. Willow is left standing alone in the middle of a half-empty hall. And it is then, in the sudden creation of space, that Willow spies it: a door, about chest-high, blended into the wall as if it were a part of the dark paneling and not an entrance to somewhere unknown.

Willow moves hesitantly toward it, pushed back by fear but drawn forward by desire. She reaches out. There is a lock, but maybe the door is open.

Her hand curls around the handle. Willow hears a soft click, but the door does not move.

And then, fingers, tight as elastic, suddenly grasp her wrist.

CHAPTER 17

"Willow."

She turns. The colonel is gripping her arm firmly. His eyes are hard. "Topher's mother would like to talk to you."

Willow's fingers drop from the handle of the locked door. Once again, she is left with questions and no answers. But this time, she won't be turned away.

"What's behind this door?" Willow asks.

"Chairs," the colonel says quickly. Too quickly. Willow is pretty sure he's lying, especially since she thinks she hears the sound of running water coming from inside.

Her frustration makes her bold. "Can I see?"

The man says nothing at first, just studies her face. "Maybe someday. It looks like your mother has come in."

He tries to pull her away, but Willow won't budge.

"How is your granddaughter, Colonel?" she can't help but ask, and even she can hear the sarcasm in her voice.

The man's eyes soften, as does his hold. He drops her arm. "She's doing nicely. Thank you for asking. Dr. Dawson says the baby will need to stay in the hospital a bit longer since he was born so early, but he will eventually be fine."

The colonel is so sincere, so honest now, that Willow's irritation immediately crumbles. Willow, of all the people in Kismet, knows that having someone you love in the hospital is never fun.

"I'm glad they're okay," she says, meaning it with all her heart.

The colonel nods. "Yes. We're very lucky. Not everyone is as ready as we are for any kind of crisis."

Willow sees that the colonel is watching Wisp across the room. Wisp is resting at that moment, but there is the ever-present tiredness in his eyes and in the bend of his back.

Wisp catches Willow looking at him and smiles widely. And she knows that for right now, he is happy and having fun.

The colonel places a hand on Willow's back and starts to gently steer her away from the little door and toward her mom and Dr. Dawson. Willow gives in this time.

"Willow," her mom says as they draw near, her eyes all merry sparkles, like sun on snow. "Come meet Topher's mother. Dr. Dawson, my daughter, Willow."

Willow turns toward Dr. Dawson. The woman's black hair is pulled back severely, soft gray sprinkled in patches throughout her braid. Her eyes are the blue of Topher's blue eye and reflect his warmth within.

"Hello, Willow," Dr. Dawson says.

She holds out a hand, and Willow takes it. Dr. Dawson's grip is firm, her handshake confident.

"I am so glad you will be here for a while," she says. "I hope I can help your mom and your brother."

Willow has heard these words before—from many doctors. They mean little to her now. They only remind her of why she is still here.

"Thanks," Willow says absently, her eyes turning back toward the door at the far end of the building. What is in that room? She needs to know.

But the colonel stands in front of it, and she can see no way around him. When he sees her looking, the colonel smiles, but he does not move. And Willow knows one thing for certain then: with the colonel here, she will not get in that room and possibly unravel this town's secret.

When they get back to Cora's, Willow tries to finally corner her mom, to find out about why she left last night and went to that building with Cora—about what Angeline has said. But her mom avoids her, saying she must call work again and talk to them about possibly taking a leave of absence. She scoots out of the room before Willow can ask her anything.

Willow looks for Wisp, to make him confess that their mom wasn't in the bedroom last night. But he is already asleep on Cora's couch, his coat and boots still on, as if he hopes to run around like that again and wants to be prepared.

Willow longs to just curl up beside Wisp, to drift, like him, into a deep late-afternoon nap. And so Willow gives in and slides herself behind him, feels him turn into her, his warmth like a medicine to her own wounded self. She pulls him closer. He settles with his head on her shoulder, one arm thrown across her middle. Willow softens toward sleep; her eyelashes fall onto her cheeks with weariness.

Willow feels like the mythical Greek Atlas, who was forced by the gods to hold up the world, day after day, keeping that weight up though he longed to set it down—just for a minute, just one tiny minute. Now Willow sets her burden down. But of course, the gods have no mercy, and neither does Wisp's illness.

Willow is wakened by wet. In the early-evening darkness, she can just make out blood on her hand. She rises carefully to her elbow to see that her brother's nose is bleeding, though he's still sleeping.

She sucks in her breath. Wisp's nosebleeds are often hard to stop. Her heart pounding, Willow slips her brother's head from her chest and goes to find her mother.

As Willow starts for the stairs, she hears voices coming from the kitchen, and so she heads there. But she is stopped before she opens the door by the words from inside.

"You will have to introduce the idea to her slowly."

It is Cora's voice, deep and raspy.

"I'm not sure she'll take to it," Mom is responding. "It's a hard concept to grasp, and one she may not like."

Cora laughs. "They all understand eventually. They all finally realize that it is best not to be caught off guard."

Willow *is* caught off guard. She stands, undecided, fear fighting her curiosity. Wisp could be in trouble, and she needs to tell her mom. But how can she not stay silent and listen to more of what is being said between Cora and her mom if answers are within her grasp at last?

"Wisp . . . ," Willow hears her mom mutter.

A coffee cup is set down with a rattle.

"Yes," Cora says. "It's time. And she'll be standing outside, so be careful not to hit her with the door."

"Oh, yes. I remember that too," her mother says.

Willow freezes, shock frozen solid from Cora's and her mom's words, like the icicles that hang off Kismet's houses.

Slowly, the kitchen door swings open, and her mom smiles at her.

"Hello, Willow. Wisp's bleeding, isn't he?"

CHAPTER 18

Willow's mom walks calmly toward the living room. Willow watches her, motionless, as if fixed to the floor.

"Aren't you going to go with her?" Cora has come from the kitchen too.

She places a hand on Willow's shoulder and gives her a little push, finally freeing Willow from where she is stuck.

Wisp. Willow runs to the living room.

Her mom is bent over her brother, shaking him gently awake. There is none of the urgency in her mom that usually accompanies these incidents. And Willow stands beside them, baffled and bewildered. Why is her mom so slow? Wisp is bleeding!

The front door opens and in come Layla and James. They have a blanket with them, and they wrap Wisp up as Willow's mom presses his nose with a towel to try to stop the bleeding.

How did they know to be here? How did Cora know she was standing outside that door?

"Come along, Willow," Mom says.

Willow follows her mom and Wisp, Layla, and James down the front walk and into the dark of a winter evening. The plow truck is waiting. And they are off quickly to the hospital. Her mom is all smiles and chats, and everyone seems just fine.

Only Willow feels panicked, and not just by Wisp.

She is dead-leaf blown away. She is corn-maze confused. What is happening? Has the world turned upside down while she slept? Why is no one on high Wisp alert?

When they arrive at the hospital, Dr. Dawson is already outside, a wheelchair all set, her blue eyes totally focused on Wisp as he is lifted from the truck.

How did Topher's mom know they were coming?

They whisk Wisp away, and Willow is left standing at the door to the emergency room.

"He'll be fine, Willow," her mom calls to her as she walks behind Dr. Dawson and the doors swing shut. "No need to worry."

Through the glass in the door, Willow watches them head down the hallway, and she feels a volcano-like boiling and burning, building just below her surface. She is standing here alone, blinking in confusion, understanding nothing.

How does her mom know Wisp will be okay? Her mother *never* assumes that.

Willow cannot solve this riddle of everyone acting so casually, this puzzle of how her mom and everyone else was ready for Wisp's nosebleed, as if they all knew.

She is tired of being the only one in this town left out of its secrets. She may not be able to go in and help Wisp, but she can do something. She can take a step toward figuring out this town's mystery, and she is determined to do it. She turns on her heel and heads for the brick building.

The front door swings open easily enough. The hall lies before her, signs for Topher's birthday decorating the walls, tables set with folded napkins, fiddles and fifes for dancing at the ready. Balloons float and bob as she closes the door behind her.

Willow walks bravely across the floor. She reaches boldly for the handle on the tiny door in the back wall. And she pulls.

Nothing. It will not open. The door is firmly closed, tightly locked.

Willow stomps her foot in anger. She lets out a cry of frustration. Lava swishes in her guts, wanting to spew out. She swallows it down.

But she refuses to stay in darkness. This door will not deter her—not now.

She sits on a folding chair and stares at the lock. She thinks and thinks on what she can do, how she can gain entrance to an explanation.

And then she remembers—Cora here, late at night, and a wall of keys that Cora guards. Could one of them unlock an answer?

She runs back to Cora's and tiptoes through the living room and the dining room to the large wooden reception desk. Upstairs, she hears Cora plodding down the hallways, sighing and muttering as she thumps along. Willow knows she must hurry if she is to escape unnoticed.

The keys are all lined up on a board of hooks, each one with a hand-painted room number, each key, with the exception of the one to Willow's room, exactly where it is meant to be. But in one corner hangs a loner, like an outcast the others do not want to associate with. It has no room number assigned, only a bright green ribbon to identify it.

It beckons Willow to it, the light from outside making it wink with welcome. Willow lifts it from its hook. Its bright green ribbon lies in her palm as if it belongs there. She hurries quickly and quietly away, the key to her questions grasped hopefully in her hands.

Back at the brick building, Willow's blood thumps loudly in her ears when she enters, but no one steps out to block her as she approaches the door. No hands reach out to stop her as she slides in the key. The lock turns easily, and the door swings open. And Willow's mouth drops in surprise.

It's a small room, but it seems larger when she looks up and sees that the ceiling is made of glass. The newly risen moon pours its light inside, illuminating corners that smell of earth and water. Hoes and handheld weeding tools, hoses, and watering cans litter the ground. In the center of the floor, the hot, supposedly magical waters of the stream trickle and bubble on their way toward Kismet's lake with its open water hole.

But at the far end of the room stands the most amazing sight. And in an instant, Willow knows that this must be the secret to Kismet.

Rising toward that glass ceiling and its promise of sky and light is a bush almost ten feet in height. Its branches are thick and full. The bush pulsates with life. It is the only greenery in the room, the only reason for all these gardening gadgets, this source of water.

But the green leafy plant is not what draws Willow inside. It is not what makes her close the door softly behind her with a tiny click.

It's the berries.

There must be hundreds of them, clustered all over its branches, dripping in grapelike bundles from the bush's every limb. In front of the bush on a small table is a bowl overflowing with those same berries—only riper, darker in color.

And they shine. Oh, how they shine.

In the bright rays of moonlight gleaming down from the ceiling, these berries twinkle an invitation, shimmering and glimmering, drawing Willow toward them.

Step closer, they seem to say. *Come. Come. Taste me.*

They are almost gold, with thin stripes of Caribbean blues and greens. Lovely to look at, they beckon her nearer, nearer.

Come. Come. Taste me.

Willow walks slowly toward the bowl of berries, their scent so enticing, like honey and lavender rolled into one. She reaches out a hand, her pulse quickening, her mouth watering.

Come. Come. Taste me.

"I wouldn't touch those if I were you," she hears behind her.

The spell is broken, and Willow turns.

Angeline stands by the door, a key in her hand.

CHAPTER 19

ngeline moves into the room. "You're not supposed to be here."

What can Willow say? There is no defense for what she has done—stolen a key, opened the door to a room where she is clearly not meant to be. But despite having behaved badly, she finds herself unwilling to give in.

"What is this place? Is this part of the big secret?" Willow demands of Angeline. "What kind of bush is that? And why is it locked in this room?"

Angeline looks Willow in the eyes. "You need to ask your mom those questions."

Willow pulls back. Angeline mentioned at the lake that her mother would decide whether she would know the secret. And she remembers that tonight, Cora told her mom that she must introduce the idea to "her" slowly. Was Cora talking about Willow? Had Angeline meant the secret was this room? Had Cora been talking about this place?

"My brother's in the hospital," Willow says. "My mom's been a little busy."

Angeline shrugs. She comes farther into the room, walks to the bowl of berries, and picks one up.

Willow watches. "What kind of berries are those? Do they taste good?"

Angeline slips the berry into her pocket. "You need to ask your mom. She'll explain it all to you. But right now, you need to leave."

Angeline tries to grab Willow's arm, but Willow wiggles away. She runs to the bowl, reaches as if to pluck a berry from the pile.

"STOP!" Angeline yells. "You have to be thirteen to eat those."

"Why?" Willow asks.

Angeline rolls her eyes. "I told you. Ask your mom."

"No," Willow says, her voice harsh and hard.

This time, she will get her answers.

Willow picks up a berry, holds it to her mouth. Her hand shakes with this bold bluff. What if the berry is poisonous? What if it kills her?

"STOP!" Angeline says again. "I told you. You're breaking the rules."

"Whose rules?" Willow says.

"The town's," Angeline answers.

"Why would a town make rules about a bush?" Willow

asks. "Are the berries dangerous? Then why did you take one? You seem okay." She holds the berry to her mouth again.

"Just stop with all the questions and give me that berry. It's not meant for you," Angeline says, holding out her hand.

Willow does as she asks. She drops the berry into Angeline's outstretched palm, but even as she does this, Willow's other fingers slip a second berry from the bowl into her coat pocket. Angeline places the first berry carefully back in the dish. Then she sighs. "Do you know what kind of trouble you would have been in if you'd eaten that?"

"No," Willow snaps, reaching threateningly toward the bowl again. "I don't. That's why I'm asking."

"Okay, okay. I'll tell you the basics, but you have to get the details from your mom. Agreed?" Angeline says.

Willow nods, pulls her hand back. The deal seems fair enough, and she has the other berry safely in her pocket.

Angeline looks down at the fruit in the bowl. "They tell you your future."

Willow blinks. "What?"

"We all know the future—or I should say, our next day," Angeline says. "I know you've been trying to figure out what makes our town so unusual, and that's it. We all know exactly what will happen the next day, and then the day after that and the day after that. Forever."

"But that's . . . well, it's . . . ," Willow stammers.

"Impossible?" Angeline answers for her. "Magic? Yeah, it is."

It seems unbelievable, what Angeline has just told her. And yet some things, strangely, begin to make sense. They click, like locks turning, pins falling into place, tightening up questions and answers into secure, sealed fixtures: the colonel knowing his granddaughter would have a baby that night, though she wasn't due for weeks; Cora making up the extra bed the first night they arrived; Layla and James finding them the night they crashed when the world was blacked out by snow; Angeline knowing she could skate; Cora telling Willow to answer the door before Topher had even knocked—all were riddles that were answered before they even became questions.

"How does it work?" Willow asks.

Angeline swirls the toe of her shoe in the dirt of the room. "Every night before we go to bed, we eat a berry. Then we fall asleep and dream about what will happen to us when we wake up the next day. And it happens just the way we dream it. You can start using the magic when you turn thirteen. Cora is the keeper of the garden. She feeds it with the water from the spring. It's the magic in the waters that lets the plant thrive, so Cora makes sure that the bush stays well fed. She picks the ripe berries early in the morning and leaves them for us in the bowl."

Willow looks at the bush—the root of Kismet's magic. The berries almost seem to wink at her.

"Is that why there are no mailboxes or phones?" Willow says as her mind processes what Angeline is telling her. "Because you already know what mail you'll get and what someone is going to say to you on the phone?"

Angeline nods. "Yeah. It's cool. Because of the magic of the berries, we save a lot of time. And it's fun. It's also why none of us ever leaves Kismet.

"So see," she says, holding out the berry she took before. "Tonight, I'll eat this berry, and I'll dream about my tomorrow. And from the berry I ate last night, I knew you would be here. I knew I would find you."

"Then why didn't you stop me before I came in?" Willow asks.

"You can't *change* the future, silly," Angeline says, smiling. "You would have gotten in whether I tried to stop you or not. It's your fate."

"Are you saying you can't change anything you dream?" Willow asks.

Angeline laughs again. "Oh, little things. Like if you know someone is going to ask you for something, you can hand it to them before they ask. Or if someone's going to get hurt, you can get them a Band-Aid before it happens. So it's not just fun, it's also useful a lot of times. But big things, no, you can't change those. If you even try, you get a terrible headache."

Willow thinks on this. What does "small things" mean? If she had a hockey game the next day, would she know when someone was going to try a shot and be able to save it? Would she know when Wisp was going to ask an embarrassing question and stop him?

Wisp!

She has completely forgotten her brother.

"I have to go," she says, more to herself than to the girl who blocks her way.

"I know." Angeline smirks even as she steps to the side.

When Willow gets to the hospital, her mother is waiting for her.

"Wisp needs to stay the night," she says. "Dr. Dawson is going to watch him. We can get him tomorrow."

Willow's mind is still reeling with all that Angeline has told her.

Some things she gets. She understands now why Layla and James were already there with the truck today: they knew Wisp would need them. And she now knows why Dr. Dawson was outside the hospital waiting for them. Dr. Dawson knew too.

But there are bigger questions that Willow still needs answers to.

"Mom?" she says, hoping to talk to her mother about what she has learned. She wonders if her mother already knows it all or if she only knows some of it. She must know a little or Cora's words in the kitchen wouldn't make sense.

"Willow," her mother says. "Please save any questions about Wisp for tomorrow. I'm too tired to talk tonight."

Willow nods, though she never meant to ask questions about Wisp. She wanted to ask about the berries. But she realizes that it's true: it's never good to approach her mother when

Wisp is ill. Now is not a good time to discuss what Willow has discovered and what her mother might know. Tomorrow, in the light of day, will be better. Her mother will be more willing to talk then.

So Willow stays silent, her mind still full of questions, trudging along behind her mother back through the snow toward Cora's. As she walks, Willow shoves her hands in her pockets. Her fingers find the berry she stole nesting there. The berry seems to radiate heat. She can almost feel its life pulse beating in her own insides. And then and there, Willow makes a decision.

Fear and exhilaration twine themselves together deep in her gut. But she won't back down. Not tonight.

Willow will figure this out on her own.

Tonight, she will pop that berry into her mouth. Tonight, she will discover just how this town's magic works. Tonight, Willow is going to dream her future.

CHAPTER 20

Willow waits for her mother to fall deep into sleep. As she lies there in the dark, her mind flits from thought to thought, worries bashing against each other like waves in a storm against a rocky coastline.

How many times has her mother warned Willow and her brother not to take chances that might put them at risk? How many times has her father told them both to use their heads? And isn't eating fruit from a supposedly magical bush, especially when you've been warned against it, a stupid idea?

Willow is no great risk taker. Before Wisp got ill, that was always his role in the family. If it were Wisp wondering about the magic of Kismet, he would have already eaten a bushel of those berries.

Not Willow. As a hockey goalie, she is constantly analyzing angles.

And yet, she is no weakling. And she wants to know the truth.

According to Angeline, the people of Kismet eat these berries all the time, every night, every day of their lives. Why would Willow be the only one to have a problem with it? Then again, she isn't thirteen. Maybe there's something important about being that age.

She wrestles with these thoughts until her mother drops into a breathing rhythm that indicates Willow could play a tuba next to their bed and her mother would dream on without so much as a twitch.

And so Willow must decide. If she is going to eat a berry and dream her next day, it must be done now. She slides from the bed and tiptoes toward where her coat hangs on a hook. She digs into the pocket and pulls the berry out. In the dim light from the bathroom down the hallway, where Cora has set a night-light for the comfort of her guests, the berry's Caribbean-colored gold-blues and greens sparkle up at Willow.

Come, they seem to say. *Come taste me.*

Willow sighs, and in that sigh, she hears her longing. The berry is beautiful, and its smell is so appealing—the mixture of lavender and honey seems to float in the air and fills her senses with a feeling of peace and comfort. She cannot help herself. The pull is too strong. Her hand lifts the berry to her mouth. She takes a deep breath, shuts her eyes, and pops it in.

The taste of the berry explodes in her mouth, surprising her with a mixture of all her favorite flavors rather than her favorite scents—chocolate and peppermint, caramel and salt. She reels from the intensity of it, overwhelmed with its sweetness. And then it hits her—hard. The drowsiness. She can feel herself being lulled, almost tugged into slumber.

She staggers back to her bed and falls down beside her mother. And she slips into a sleep so deep and so vivid that she knows, even as she tumbles into it, that she will long for it again when she wakes.

The dream the berries bring is bright and runs quickly through her head. She wakes and dresses, chatting with her mother. Though she cannot hear the exact words they are saying, she senses their harmony, sees her mother's reaction to her words. She sees herself helping Cora prepare breakfast. As Willow moves about the kitchen, her foot finds a puddle of water. She falls down hard, wincing as her hip hits the floor. Later, she and her mother head to the hospital, Willow still favoring one hip. But the pain seems to disappear when she sees that Wisp is all smiles and ready to go home. It takes a few hours, but at last, they head back. Topher is with them, and he and his mother help Willow and her mom get Wisp settled again at Cora's.

But the day ends with a surprise—one that, even in her dream-filled state, makes Willow squirm with embarrassment. And even as she turns and mumbles in her sleep, she asks herself: *Will this really happen tomorrow? Will I really do that?*

Willow wakes, relieved to find that she is still alive and that the berry wasn't poisonous. She is ready to see if it is truly magical. Willow normally can't remember her dreams, but today she remembers every detail—even the one that curls her toes and makes a pit form in her stomach.

As she lies in bed, it suddenly occurs to her why Cora always says "Sweet dreams" at the end of the night, why Layla called the same thing to them on their first night in Kismet. Willow almost laughs as she thinks of this.

When her mom wakes, Willow rises with her. They chat as they dress, just as Willow dreamt. There is a feeling of comfort in watching her mother move about the room in a way Willow has already foreseen, performing tasks she already knows her mother will do. There is a sense of relief, knowing that today, at least, she and her mother will not fight. Her berry dream has brought about a wonderful sense of restfulness, and she eats it up like pudding on a spoon.

They head downstairs, finding Cora in the kitchen. Cora smiles at Willow, just as Willow knew she would. Cora hands Willow a grapefruit, and Willow sections her half. As she goes to grab a plate, she pauses. She remembers her dream last night, the way she fell and hurt her hip.

So she walks slowly to the table. After all, if she knows beforehand that she is to fall, why not stop it from happening? Isn't that the beauty of the berry?

When she sees the water, she simply steps around the puddle waiting to trip her up. She almost laughs out loud with surprise and delight when she doesn't slip.

The day progresses just as Willow knows it will. And she

finds that she enjoys knowing what is to come. It is like reading a beloved book for the tenth time and finding an old friend there again.

She likes knowing James and Layla will pick them up, offering them a ride, as she and her mother trudge through the snow toward the hospital late in the afternoon. She likes knowing she will see the colonel snowshoeing his way around town, and that he will salute them as they drive by.

She finds she is more patient at the hospital, knowing what is to come. Where normally, the amount of paperwork that accompanies Wisp's release from a hospital drives her almost mad, the time it takes today barely registers.

She and Wisp play several games of Clue as they wait to be cleared. Of course, Willow already knows who the killer is, so she needs not wait the entire round to make a guess and win. She almost laughs out loud when she sees Wisp's frustration. He can't figure out how she can keep guessing correctly so early in the game.

The nurse stops by to see what Wisp wants for dinner.

"He'll have the chicken soup," Willow says.

"Hey," Wisp says. "How did you know that's what I wanted?"

Willow taps her head and grins. "Just smart, I guess."

She thinks of all the other ways she can surprise Wisp down the road if she continues to eat these berries. She can hand him clothes he wants to wear before he asks. She can play the magician and tell him the suit and number of a card he holds in his hand. She cannot wait to baffle and amaze him.

After supper, their mom comes in the room. All the paper-work has been completed. Evening falls as they pack Wisp up and prepare to take him home.

Dr. Dawson offers to drive them. When Topher arrives to help, Willow's mouth goes dry as she meets his eyes. In all the excitement over knowing her day, she forgot her evening.

"Wisp is going to be all right," Topher tells her as they push him in a wheelchair and follow Willow's mom and Dr. Dawson toward the hospital exit. "I promise."

He does not need to promise. As Cora once knew, Willow too knows that Wisp will be fine today. Still, she appreciates Topher's trying to soothe her.

They all climb into the Dawsons' SUV and drive back to Cora's. Willow helps Dr. Dawson and her mother carry Wisp upstairs.

Finally, they get Wisp settled.

"Go on downstairs, Willow," her mom says. "Keep Topher company. It's late, but Dr. Dawson has a few things to do here before we're finished."

"It's okay," Willow says quickly. "I can help you."

She is nervous about what she saw in her dream last night.

"No," her mother says. "Go on down. Don't leave Topher alone."

"Should I wake Cora?" Willow asks. Cora shuffling around downstairs might change things.

Her mother shakes her head. "Absolutely not. Let that woman sleep. Now go."

Willow avoided slipping today. She guessed the Clue murderer again and again before she had all the cards in her hand. Maybe she can change this part of the night too. But does she want to? She's not sure.

Slowly, Willow walks down the stairs. Topher smiles at her, and her heart beats, beats.

"I'm glad Wisp's okay," Topher says to Willow.

Willow looks him in the eye, assessing. "You knew it would be all right. Did you eat your berry last night?"

Topher's mouth drops open. "My mom told me your mom hadn't told you about that yet."

"I have other sources," Willow says, but she does not elaborate. She isn't about to tell him that she is a thief, given to breaking in where she isn't wanted, stealing and eating things she isn't meant to eat.

Topher lets out a laugh. "Well then, you should know. I'm not thirteen yet."

"Oh, but you are," she says, laughing. "You're thirteen right now. It's twelve-oh-one."

At her words, Topher's face falls, and Willow stands there, puzzled, as she was last night when she dreamt this, as to why that might be.

"Aren't you glad it's your birthday?" she asks. "Aren't you glad to be part of a town that knows its future?"

Topher bites his lip. "Sure," he says.

But Willow can hear uncertainty in his voice, and for some

reason she can't fathom, she sees sadness in his eyes, as she did last night in her visions.

He sighs. "I'm sorry. I'm just tired. Great way to start a birthday celebration day, eh?"

Willow feels her face redden. She has seen herself do it in the dream. She knows it will make him happy. But still she hesitates, backing away a bit to think.

But as she does, a pain shoots through her head, a pain so intense she almost cannot catch her breath.

Topher moves closer to her. "Willow, are you okay?"

With his nearness, the pain in her head begins to subside a bit.

And Willow realizes in that moment that this must be one of those "big things" Angeline was talking about, the ones that cannot be changed, the ones that give you terrible headaches. The berry has predicted this fate for her. She cannot escape it.

She takes a deep breath, knowing it will be all right. He will not reject her. The berry has shown her how delighted he will be. And yet she still grows warm as she steps toward Topher, shaking with nervousness.

The pain in her head lessens as she places her hands on Topher's shoulders and lifts herself up on her tippy-toes.

And the pain completely disappears as she gives Topher Dawson a kiss. Right there. Right in Cora's hallway, Willow kisses a boy.

"Happy birthday, Topher," Willow whispers.

"Wow," Topher breathes with surprise, finally smiling, as Willow knew he would. "Wow."

And Willow knows that while she may have been nervous, perhaps the berry was right. Willow has given Topher Dawson a perfect first gift for his thirteenth birthday.

CHAPTER 21

After everyone leaves, Willow runs on light feet up the stairs to her bedroom, her mind all Topher-sodden.

Her mother has fallen asleep in a chair, exhaustion lines etched on her face. Tomorrow, they will have some deep discussing to do, now that Willow knows the magic of Kismet.

"Willow?"

It is Wisp, awake, as she had known he would be. Willow goes to his side, and he swings open his blanket. Willow slides in next to him. Wisp puts his head on her chest, and Willow sighs. Though she didn't hear the next words that are to be said, she knows from the way she looked in her berry dream that the next conversation is going to be a tough one, one that will make her sad.

They lie there for a while, all soft breathing, all brother-sister coziness.

"I want to go home," Wisp finally whispers into the dark, and Willow's free-flying heart is brought abruptly back to its cage. "I'm so tired of all these tests and things."

"I know," she says, still wishing to dodge this conversation. But when she even thinks about avoiding it, the pain in her head begins again.

"I miss Dad," Wisp says.

"I do too," Willow says. "I'll call him tomorrow and see if he'll come up here."

Even as she says this, she doubts her father will override her mother and drive up. But the pain in her head subsides even more, giving her sweet relief. And she knows now that the magic is not going to let her change this conversation either. She has promised her brother something she doubts their father will deliver, but still, she will try. She is fated to have this talk with her brother, like it or not. This conversation is not a "little thing."

"Yes, please," Wisp says.

Willow feels her brother's tense limbs loosen beside her, and she realizes that perhaps it is for the best. Today, she has given two gifts away: the gift of a first kiss to Topher and the gift of a promise to Wisp.

"Don't you want to go home too?" Wisp asks.

Willow bites her lip. Does she want to go home? If he'd asked her last night, she would have said yes. Now she is not so sure. Seeing your future is alluring, and would certainly relieve a lot of the stress their family feels these days.

"I don't know," Willow says. "It's kind of nice here."

"It's not that I don't like it here a lot. It's just I'm so . . . ," Wisp says, then pauses. ". . . tired," he finishes.

"I know," Willow manages to choke out.

"I wish . . ." He stops again.

"What?" Willow asks. If her brother wants anything she can get him, she will move mountains to do it.

"I wish she'd stop," he says wearily. "I wish I could find a way to make her stop trying."

Willow's heart breaks in silence. There is nothing she can do to bring him this—this unachievable thing that he most wants. If her dad could not convince her mother, Willow has no chance. All she can do is offer him sisterly support, sibling understanding.

"Me too," Willow whispers to him. "Me too."

Wisp lays his head against her, closes his eyes.

Their talk is over. Willow knows they will say nothing more. She saw that last night in her dream. This day is finally done. She has lived it twice.

And now that it is over, Willow has to admit that seeing your day ahead of time is a pretty good thing. Knowing that she was to give Topher Dawson a kiss made doing it easier, even if she was nervous. And now, with Wisp, with this talk that she knew would be hard, she feels less sad than she would have if it had taken her completely off guard. Knowing something awful or scary is coming, even if you can't avoid it, makes the hurt a bit more bearable and gives you courage to face it.

Willow thinks back over everything that day, the good and

the bad. And she realizes that she has liked the knowing, the certainty, the relief in seeing ahead of time what will come, in having the ability to be prepared. And she thinks she understands now why people eat a berry every night and why they never want to leave Kismet.

CHAPTER 22

Willow wakes just before dawn. It is still dark outside, but there is a whisper of light against the sky. The wind has picked up. It moans its way into Cora's house, tapping bent branches against windows, swirling softened snow against sashes. But Willow doesn't think it is the wind that has roused her from sleep.

She lies still. And then she sees a shadow move slowly, stealthily in the light of the doorway. Willow catches her breath. Is her mom leaving them alone again to meet Cora? Will Willow finally get a chance to confront her?

But a quick glance to her left tells Willow that she is wrong. Her mom is still there, under the blankets of their bed, lost in slumber and unaware.

So who is it creeping about the house just as the sun approaches?

Cora is not a reckless woman, even in this town she knows so well. She double-locks every door and window at night when she goes to bed.

Willow knows she should scream—do something to wake her mom and alert her—but she is frozen with fear.

She wishes she'd had another berry to eat. Then she would know who it is and what to do. She longs for a second chance at that magic, its sweet taste and ability to reveal the future.

But at last, in the wan light from the window, she sees that the person skulking outside their bedroom door is Topher. What is he doing here?

If her mom wakes and finds Topher sneaking about, she may freak out—or not. She should, but Willow can't anticipate her mother's reactions at all anymore. For all Willow knows, her mom would welcome him with her newly minted smile.

Whatever her mom may do, Willow knows enough to stay still. Topher tiptoes into the bedroom. He puts a finger to his lips when he sees that she is awake and motions to her clothes. With a hook of his finger, he invites her to follow him.

Willow's curiosity prickles with possibilities. What can Topher want at this time in the morning?

If she'd eaten a berry, she'd know. Now she will have to follow him to find out.

Willow slides away from Wisp as Topher slips from the room. When she is dressed, she sneaks down the stairs, hurries through the darkened living room. She finds him waiting in the hallway. He has written a note, which he hands to her along with a pen.

Gone out with Topher. Be back soon.

Willow hesitates, thinking of Wisp and how angry her mother will be with her for stealing away like this, going off to do something impulsive, without telling her first.

"Come on," Topher whispers, his lips close to her ear. "Let's do something totally unpredictable."

Willow looks up at him, sees a smile twitch the corners of his lips. She knows that if she does this, she will be in big trouble. But rebellion over a life often put on hold rises from her gut. And it is Topher's birthday, after all. Perhaps, she can even get more answers to some of the questions she still has about the berries.

Willow takes the pen. With a flourish, she signs her name.

He sets the note on the table in the front hall and hands her her coat and mittens and ski boots.

Willow grins, putting her worry aside. After all, she has already stolen and eaten a berry. What could be worse?

Outside, Topher picks up a backpack and shrugs it on. He has cross-country skis waiting for both of them, sitting side by side. Willow slides on the skis that go with the boots he gave her inside and follows him out onto the road and into the near dark. The cold nips at her fingers and toes, but they are both laughing so hard as they make their daring escape that Willow hardly feels anything but delight.

Soon they are winging their way down the deserted main street of Kismet. The snow on the road is hard packed and perfect for going quickly and silently. They ski past all the darkened homes, the locked-up shops, the movie theater and hospital.

At last, they reach the far edge of town.

Light sharpens the horizon, turning the sky ahead of them all pink and puffy and full of promise. At a fork in the road, Topher takes the less traveled path. They are climbing steeply now, up and away from Kismet.

Willow is breathing heavily, as is Topher. It is a long climb to the top of the hill. As they approach the summit, a sign reading LEAVING KISMET seems to shimmer into view. It greets them in big, bold lettering, along with a wire fence and an iron gate. The barriers hem them in, but Topher opens the gate easily enough with a key, and they glide through, past the sign to the very top of the mountain.

"Wow," Willow says, bending over and gasping for breath. "I am really out of shape."

Topher laughs. "Yes, getting up here is hard. But now we're free!" he shouts to the wind as they stand at the top of the hill, the gate still open, looking down at Kismet, the brick building, and Cora's house far, far in the distance.

Willow laughs, even as a shiver of anticipation shimmies down her spine.

And she wonders what the day will hold.

They turn from the top and Willow is surprised to see a bridge now, one she did not notice when they slipped through the gate. Topher locks the gate behind them and then they are off again, sliding across the bridge on their skis and down a long hill.

They ski to the forest floor, and then Topher turns back toward town, following a wooded path. After ten minutes of wending their way down the trail, they come upon a narrow road. They ski along this road for about a mile, until finally, Topher stops.

In front of them is a cabin.

"This was my father's little hideaway," he says. "No one knew about it but us. It's on the same lake that we skated on in Kismet, but way on the other side. My father used to bring me here all the time, but I haven't been in a while."

"Where's your father now?" Willow asks.

Topher frowns. "I'm not sure. We've lost touch. Not having phones in Kismet kind of makes communication with someone from 'away' a bit tough."

"I'm sorry," Willow says, and she is. She can't imagine not even knowing where her father is.

"Not a topic for today," Topher says, ending any further discussion. "It's my birthday, so all unhappy thoughts are taboo."

Willow nods. He is right. She shouldn't make him feel sad today.

The wind is strong on this side of the lake, and there is only a dusting of snow. Kismet now lies under blankets and blankets of the stuff, but this little slice of woodland is winter whiteless.

Topher slides off his skis and his backpack. "Ready to try ice boating?"

"Ice boating?" Willow asks.

Topher smiles and nods toward the lake. Through the trees, Willow sees a sailboat sitting on the snow near the shore.

"We're going to sail on ice?" she asks.

"Yep. Do you want to try?"

"Sure," Willow says. She feels wild and a bit reckless, and it's a good, good feeling.

Topher laughs. "I thought you might. Have you ever sailed before?"

"No," Willow tells him.

"Then I'll teach you. Come on. Let's get out there. Just let me drop my stuff off." Topher opens the front door to the cabin and carries his backpack inside. Willow follows.

The cottage has four large rooms—a living room, kitchen, and two bedrooms. There is a log-beamed ceiling and a fieldstone fireplace, and lots of crannies for curling up and nooks for napping. But there are also cobwebs everywhere, hanging from the rafters and the furniture, proving that indeed, no one has been here in some time.

It's warmer inside, but Willow's breath still smokes out in tiny gusts of moist air.

Topher places his bag on the counter. "Okay. Let's go sailing."

As Willow follows him outside, all thoughts of magic and berries and missing fathers are forgotten in the excitement of trying something new.

The lake is like glass, smooth and black.

"It's not often we get these kinds of conditions," Topher says. "I can't believe our luck. It must be birthday luck." He looks out at the ice and then at her. "Or because you came."

Willow smiles, then reddens as she realizes she probably looks like an idiot the way she is grinning at him.

She helps him push the boat onto the ice. There are three blades on the bottom of the boat. Topher explains that they will ride those blades over the frozen water, just like skates.

He has Willow hop on and then gets on himself, the two of them scrunched together tightly on the seat, and he raises the sail. The wind roars beside them and picks them up in its grasp. Their little boat responds with a groan, and they begin moving, faster and faster, until soon they are flying over the ice, the wind hurtling them across the lake.

Willow holds on to the sides of the seat. Her eyes tear up from the wind, and her heart beats crazily from the speed. Yet she can't help but laugh with delight. Topher lets out a shout of joy that mixes with the roar of the blades on the ice and the wail of the lines from the sail as it is pulled taut. His face is flushed. His eyes dance with joy. He is captain of this lake, and Willow is his first mate.

Topher tightens the sail even more just as the wind twists and turns. Soon they are on the edge of only two blades, and zooming faster than Willow has ever moved on skates. Fear pumps deep in her stomach, but Willow pushes it away. *Be brave,* she tells herself as they sail straight toward trees and land.

Topher pulls up just short of crashing on the far shore.

They lean back, their cheeks chafed with cold, their hands frozen to lines and sides. Both of them happy.

"Were you scared?" he finally asks her.

Willow forces herself to shrug, though her mouth is dry and her heart beats a rock-n-roll drum rhythm. "No," she says as casually as she can.

Topher laughs. "Liar."

Willow grins. "Okay. Maybe a little."

"Come on, then," Topher says. "You try now."

He hands her the line that controls the sail, showing her how to judge where the wind is coming from and how to catch those gusts that will move the boat across the ice. He sits behind her, steering the boat, his mittened hand on hers as she controls the sail, and once more they fly across the lake.

And just as they start to really move, the sail quivering and straining against the wind, the sun bursts from the clouds and lights up the lake in a dawning that makes Willow ache with love of this world.

And even though today is Topher's birthday, Willow feels like it's hers too.

CHAPTER 23

They shoot across the lake for almost two hours, swooping from one side to the other, each time trying to top their own speed record.

Finally, Topher slides the little boat close to shore, drops the sail, and helps Willow off.

"I'm starving," he says. "We should probably head back."

Willow laughs. "I agree. My stomach is growling louder than those blades on that ice and the wind together."

They pull the boat onto the shore, tie it up, and then head into the cabin.

Immediately, Willow's fingers and toes start to burn as blood rushes back into them in the relative warmth of the cabin. Topher goes to grab his backpack. "I brought some granola bars to tide us over until we get home."

"You're not going to cook me something?" Willow teases.

Topher shrugs. "Actually, I can cook, at least a little. When you're being raised by a single parent who works a full-time job and you've got two hungry little brothers, yeah, you learn to cook. What about you?"

"I can cook too," Willow tells him. "When your brother is sick, and your mom is running around trying to find out what's wrong with him, yeah, you learn to cook—at least a little."

She has a sudden memory of cooking with Wisp when he was younger, making special meals for their mom and dad. But those meals were for fun, not because she had to, not because her mother was too busy with Wisp to make anything for them to eat.

Topher hands her a granola bar.

Willow unwraps it, the simple act of pulling away the paper giving her the courage to tell him what she is thinking. "My brother and I used to love to cook dinner for my mom and dad. Wisp would always slow down and be more patient if he was allowed to hold a knife and chop something up." She forces a laugh. "I think my mom welcomed the break from chasing him around all day back then."

"You don't do that anymore?" Topher asks.

Willow shakes her head. "No. He can't really eat a lot with his illness. Why would he want to cook what he can't have?"

"Or do you think maybe it's because Wisp thinks you've lost interest in cooking with him?" Topher asks.

Willow is about to say no but remembers how Wisp's friends stopped wanting to hang out with him when he got sick. Has she done that to Wisp too?

Topher shoves his granola bar wrapper in the backpack. "Yeah, well, we should get back before your mom gets too mad at me."

Willow agrees. She opens the door so they can grab their skis. And she catches her breath.

Outside the cabin window, Willow can see nothing but white. A storm has engulfed them.

"What are we going to do?" she asks.

"We can't go back in this," Topher says, looking out the cabin door. "It would be too easy to get lost. I have to find the bridge and then the gate to get back in, and we might miss them with this snow."

Realizing they are stranded there for a while, they go back inside the cabin. Topher pulls out some cards. They play hearts and gin and go fish and any other card game they can think of to still the nervousness they both feel at being stuck.

Willow thinks of Wisp and how horrible it is that she doesn't have a phone to tell him or her mom where she is and that she's safe. She bites her lip with guilt.

"We're going to miss the party," Topher says as he frowns and glances out the window before dealing more cards. "My mom is going to be so mad."

Willow sighs, knowing how much trouble they both will be in. Their moms and Kismet may never forgive them.

It is cold in the cabin, but there is nothing to be done about it. They are afraid to start a fire, and at least it's a little warmer than outside. Willow shivers as they sit there, waiting for the storm to end.

At last, she can stand it no longer. If they can't dig their way out of this predicament, Willow will at least try to dig up more facts about the magic in Kismet.

"Topher," she says, and she keeps her voice quiet and steady, hoping it sounds like a trustworthy voice, "can you tell me more about the berries?"

Topher looks up, startled. "I thought you knew everything."

Willow shakes her head. "Not *everything*."

Topher looks everywhere but at her. "We're not supposed to tell. Your parents are the only ones who are supposed to explain everything."

Frustration floats up inside Willow again. "Stop," she says. "We're stuck here, and my mom has enough to worry about. I want to hear it from you. Please, Topher."

He hesitates and then shrugs. "Do you know the history of the berries? I can at least tell you that."

Willow shakes her head.

He looks out the window for a moment and then begins. "The story of the berries actually starts back in the seventeen hundreds sometime. I don't know the exact date. Sorry. I don't remember things like that." He looks at Willow apologetically, as if an exact date will make a difference. "It was about the time when my ancestors, the Acadians, left Canada. Some of them landed here looking for a new life. A couple named Fabre came and began panning for gold in the waters by the lake. One day, the woman was down there . . ."

Here Topher sweeps his hand in the direction of the lake on which they just sailed. "She was near where we skated a few nights ago, washing her clothes, when she saw this bush. The berries looked really good, and so she ate one. She immediately fell asleep and had the most vivid dream. When she woke, she was completely refreshed, and she went home. The next day, her dream came true. Exactly as she had dreamt it, her day unfolded. It kind of spooked her, so she brought a berry to her husband, and he ate it that night. And he had a dream of *his* next day that also came true."

Topher shrugs. "Anyway, they thought this was better than gold. And so they left our village and started riding around from town to town, offering the berries to people who would pay. And each of these people had a vision of exactly what would happen to them the next day, and the Fabres grew rich offering people the chance to know their fate for the day. But it was kind of a dumb idea."

"Why?" Willow asks. "People would pay a lot to know what their future is."

Topher nods. "Yeah, they did, until someone said the Fabres were witches and that was that. The couple were tried, sentenced, and hanged."

Willow blinks with surprise.

Topher laughs. "I guess in all their excitement to make money and show everybody else what would happen to them the next day, they forgot to eat their own berries and see their next day—like I said, pretty dumb. They could have at least known it was coming."

"What happened after that?" Willow asks.

"Not much," Topher says. "Nobody found the bush again until, I think it was 1862. That's when Grace's great-, like three or four times back, grandfather found it. He was about ten and down fishing by the lake near the open water hole and discovered it.

"Anyway," he continues, "this great-grandfather took his own father down to the lake to show it to him. There were these old legends about the bush, rumors, so when Grace's great-grandfather's father saw it, he was kind of shocked but also pretty willing to accept its abilities. So, like the dumb Fabres, he set himself up for business. He dug up the bush and replanted it in his backyard. He watered the plant with waters from the lake and picked the ripe berries every day. And he sold them to people so they could see their next day.

"Of course," Topher adds, grimacing, "by 1862 there were no more witch hunts, so he was fairly safe doing that. But what he hadn't counted on was the war. You know, the Civil War."

Willow nods. "Yeah, I know about the Civil War. But what does a war have to do with anything?"

"Well," Topher tells her, "a lot of people were losing their sons and husbands. And every family got really anxious, wanting to know if the papers the next day would announce that their son or father or boyfriend had been killed. . . ."

In Topher's pause, Willow has a sudden vision of Wisp. And it hits her hard. If her mom knew she could face a day with the certainty that Wisp would be okay, she would pay the stars and the moon to have that peace of mind—even if it was only for twenty-four hours. Now she realizes why they might be staying in Kismet for a while.

"But what Grace's great-grandfather didn't count on was the frenzy of these people. They wanted to know before the sun rose—was their son or husband alive? And in all the chaos and clamoring and people shoving and pushing and chasing him to get a berry, he was murdered, and the bush was torn to shreds."

"So how did you get it back?" Willow asks.

Topher gives her a slight smile. "In 1962—exactly a hundred years later—someone found it down by the lake, growing just as tall and large as you please, right where the waters meet. Remember I told you they were magical?"

"It just grew up again?" Willow asks in disbelief.

He nods. "Yep. But this time around, the town council laid claim to it. And they built that brick building and transplanted it there and controlled the berries. They knew the dangers now and the possibility of its being discovered by the world—the craziness that might ensue. They didn't want that. They wanted a cohesive town that believed in the magic. So while they realized that the berries gave a lot of people comfort in an uncertain world, they felt they should be offered to everyone for free. They built a wall around the town and put up gates and kept the bush locked up. Now everyone who wants that peace of mind has his or her own set of keys and can pick up a berry anytime during the day once they turn thirteen. Everyone eats it at night, so your dreams of the next day coincide with your regular sleeping patterns, and we don't fall asleep during normal daylight hours. And the bush has been here for over fifty years now," he finishes.

"What did you mean 'everyone who wants that peace of mind'?" Willow asks. "Can you choose whether you want to eat the berries or not?"

"In a way . . . ," he says slowly.

"What way?" Willow asks him.

"Well, it starts, like I told you, when you're little," Topher says, his voice stiff like a tightened violin bow. "Occasionally, your parents reveal something to you. And you are kind of amazed and you begin to wonder how they knew something before it even happened. . . . Then when you turn twelve, there's a little ceremony in each kid's house, and your parents finally tell you the truth—basically what I've just told you. After that, the serious stuff sets in. They begin to tell you more of your next day, things you'll experience in common. Like your mom might pour the cereal you want without you even asking her for it."

Willow remembers Cora giving her grapefruit juice the first morning they arrived in Kismet. Now she sees how Cora knew.

"It kind of freaks you out," Topher continues, "having parts of your life unfold the way they told you it would, seeing your-self do things they said you would do. For a week, they let you eat a berry before bed and see what it's like."

Willow realizes that yesterday she did just that.

"And then," he says, "they tell you about the choice."

"The choice?" Willow asks.

"When you're thirteen, you have to choose," Topher says softly. "Stay in Kismet and know your future, or leave."

"You can't stay here if you won't?"

Topher shakes his head. "They want a town living together in harmony, believing that knowing your day ahead of time is important. So you have to take a pledge to the town if you want to stay, agreeing to eat a berry and follow your fate for the day."

"And if you choose to not eat a berry every day?" she asks.

"Then you . . ." He pauses, sadness filling his features. "You have to leave Kismet permanently."

CHAPTER 24

Willow stares at him. "You mean you have to choose between knowing your future every day or leaving your family forever?"

He nods, and his mouth curls down. "You're supposed to think about your decision from the time you turn twelve until you make your choice at thirteen. If you leave, like my father did, you can't come back."

"But that's ridiculous," Willow says. "How can they prevent you from coming back?"

Topher looks at her. "The locked gate? The bridges that give you access to the town? They both can keep you out. One you need a key for. The other, over the years, has become harder and harder for outsiders to find. Did you not notice that the bridge is difficult to see?"

Willow thinks on this. She remembers the night they arrived. She and her mom had not seen the bridge at all. She thought then that the snow had been coming down too hard.

But today—yes, even today, she did not see the bridge when they first left the town.

"How can the bridges do that?" she asks. "Appear and disappear like that?"

Topher shrugs. "The magic of the waters that feed the bush and make the berries. The bridges appear to all of us from Kismet, and to people who are meant to come here. But they aren't always visible to people who aren't welcome."

"Do you think we were meant to come here?" Willow asks.

"I think there was a reason for letting us bring you in," Topher says.

"What are you going to do?"

Topher's face is anguished. "I don't know. I've thought about it this whole year, and I still don't know what to do. I mean, I love my brothers and my mother and living in Kismet. But the idea of knowing what the next day will hold, and the next day after that, and the day after that, with no surprises . . . well, I don't want that either. It seems so . . . so boring."

Willow has always heard that there are two sides to every story. And suddenly, in that moment, she sees how dreaming your future every night wouldn't always be a good thing. Yesterday had been fun, knowing what was to come, but maybe that would get old if it happened every day.

She thinks about her day today. If she had known what was to happen ahead of time, would she have felt the same incredible happiness?

Angeline might have been right—there was a good point to

it all. But Topher has gotten to the heart of the argument. How can you enjoy life if you always know what happens next?

"If you refuse to join Kismet, where would you go?" Willow asks.

"One person from Kismet is always on the outside," Topher says. "That person lives in the real world and handles working and getting food and clothing for the community. The job rotates. Everybody does one year on the outside. Right now, there's a woman named Annie out there. She takes any kids who don't want to stay."

"Why don't you just go live with your dad?" Willow asks.

Topher sighs. "I told you. I haven't heard from my dad in a while. The last I knew, he was living outside Boston. But I'm not a hundred percent sure he's still there."

"Can't you call him from Cora's?" Willow asks.

Topher shakes his head. "That phone is only for the colonel to contact our outside person and place orders or give directions or—for people like you, ones who might join Kismet."

Willow shudders now when Topher says this.

"Not that there have been any new people here since I can remember," Topher adds bitterly. "And I'm really sorry you even had to *hear* about all this."

"Why don't you run away and tell someone? I'm sure somehow you could find a way back," Willow says, her mind searching for escape plans, daring schemes, a trick that will help Topher avoid this prison of a decision.

He shakes his head again. "Someone tried that—twenty

years ago. This boy named Harry stole a key and escaped without making a decision. And he went and talked to a reporter, told him the whole thing. And he brought the reporter back. But he wasn't able to find the bridge. Eventually, he gave up and the reporter left, thinking Harry was just crazy. And as soon as the reporter was gone, the bridge appeared. Harry never left Kismet again."

He looks at her. "That's fate, Willow. You can't escape what is planned for your life. You can't beat your fate. No one can."

"What if you just absolutely refuse to make a choice and insist on staying?" Willow asks, her voice rising with this new idea, her mind imagining Topher taking a stand, beginning a battle.

"You're not allowed to stay," Topher said. "It's that simple. They force you out, take away your key to get back in. And as I said, if you don't have a key, you can't open the gate, and finding the bridge has become really difficult. It's almost as if the waters are making this town more invisible every day, as if we are fated to not ever leave here at all. That scares me too."

"Angeline says you can change little things," Willow says. "Why don't you just stay here and change your day every day the way you want it to be?"

"You can only change *really* little things," Topher says, "like we don't have to reread mail we've already read in our dream so we don't even bother delivering it. And if we know something is about to happen, we can prepare for it somewhat—like Old Woman Wallace knowing what you'll eat and having it ready before you order it. But the big things—those are the ones that if you try to change them, you struggle physically. People who've tried get terrible headaches that they say are unbearable. If you try to change too much of what fate has in store for you, you literally can't hold your head up. It's not a way anyone would want to live. Besides, the town wants everyone to agree not to change anything anyway. They all want the certainty and predictability."

Willow thinks about the headaches she had last night when she tried to change a few things. They were incredibly painful. She imagines that living with such agony for any extended amount of time would be impossible.

Topher sighs. "I've tried to come up with an idea to escape this decision, Willow. But there's no way out. I'm stuck."

Willow's stomach churns as she thinks about Topher's situation. On the one hand, there is the feeling of comfort and reassurance that comes from knowing what is ahead. But to do that every day? To already know you'd win a game would be awesome. But to know every Christmas what your gifts would be before you open them would pretty much ruin the day. So which would she choose?

She thinks about today again—all its lovely surprises. And she knows then which she would opt for: she would choose unpredictability over knowing. But for Topher, that choice means leaving his family and Kismet.

Where yesterday she had enjoyed knowing what her future was for the day, today Willow is truly glad not to be a part of this berry-eating, fate-knowing town. Still, she is a fighter. She's not about to give up.

"There has to be some way around this, Topher," she says. "Maybe together, we can think of something."

Topher smiles, but it's a sad smile. "I don't have much time, though. I'm supposed to be deciding tonight, at the party."

He gets up and looks out the window. "The snow's stopped."

Willow stands there and looks out too, thoughts of the berries and magical waters shoved to the back of her mind. Topher is right. The sun is almost setting. It is a fine line on the horizon, pushing a sliver of light through the remaining black clouds.

"What do you think we should do?" Topher says, and for once his savvy sureness is gone. "It's going to get kind of dark out there soon. We won't be able to find our way easily. If we miss the gate, we could be in real trouble."

But Willow knows they have to get back. She may be able to escape her mother for a few hours, but all night is another story.

"We have to try," she says.

"Okay," Topher says, frowning. "We'll head back."

Slowly, they put on their coats, hats, and mittens, each reluctant to leave. Topher finds a flashlight in a drawer.

They are lucky. The batteries work, so they will have some light to help them find their way.

They step out into the newly whitewashed but darkening world.

Willow knows she is going to be in a lot of trouble.

"Stay close," Topher says. "I'm going to try to follow the road the whole way around rather than the wooded path, even though it will take us longer."

Willow nods. She prays that leaving the cabin is the right decision. What if they get lost? Today, she has no way of knowing.

But she can't let these thoughts hold them back. They have to plow on—through snow and darkness—back to Kismet and their waiting families.

CHAPTER 25

Cold sneaks into the small open slices of skin at her wrists and the sliver exposed at the base of her neck. The night is blackest black, and the flashlight Topher holds floats like some ghostly spirit over the snow as they push themselves on what he thinks is the road back home. Soon her arms and legs shake with fatigue, and Willow is unsure how much longer she can keep going in this dark and white world.

She tries not to let fear bury her thoughts any deeper than her skis sink into this fresh carpet of snow. But it is difficult not to feel a rising panic—much like the rising wind that whips about them now, drawing the storm away with it.

What if they made a mistake leaving the cabin? What if they are headed not toward Kismet but toward more wilderness? If she'd eaten a berry, she'd know if they were going to be okay. She'd know how mad her mom will be.

And that leads her mind in its swirling circles back to Wisp.

What if he got really ill while she was gone? The guilt of wishing for normal, the guilt of wishing for anything, washes over her. She knows it is Wisp who needs all the luck. It chews on her heart and her head, and she pushes herself harder to try to outrun it.

Up they climb. Willow prays that this is a good sign, for didn't they go up and down on their way to the cabin?

But nothing looks familiar. And how could it? Trees all look alike with their similar bare branches, each one weighted with matching snow.

She passes tree after tree on a path she hopes is a road, following a boy and a flashlight and these trees, which even now may be misleading them in their quest to find Kismet.

They drive on, her breath coming out in misty clouds, the sky above them slowly clearing, starlight announcing the end of the day.

At last, they crest the hill. In front of them, the bridge shimmers into view, and beyond, the gate offers them a welcome. In the rising moonlight, they can see that they have reached their destination.

Main Street is quiet. The snowbanks encase them as they enter the town. Willow has no idea what time it is, but from the hunger pangs she feels and the darkness that surrounds them, she would guess it's past dinner.

When Willow's footsteps echo on the first step of the porch, Cora's front door flies open. Her mother stands there, in the warmth of the doorway, arms crossed, a look frostier than the windowpanes of these town houses frozen onto her face.

"Yep, I'm in trouble," Willow whispers to Topher, though fear and relief twine together in her gut. If Wisp were ill, her mom would not be angry with her. She would be too focused on Wisp. And so Willow knows that Wisp is probably safely inside.

"Topher," her mother says. "I believe your mother is looking for you."

Topher sighs. "You may be in trouble," he whispers back to Willow. "But nothing like I will be. I've ruined my party." He steps away. "Later?"

Willow nods and hands her poles and skis back to Topher. And then she goes to face her punishment.

Her mother's lecture is fast and furious.

Willow tries to explain about the cabin and the snow and how they only meant to go for a few hours and not for an entire day. Her mom listens but does not excuse Willow's brash behavior.

Finally, she tells Willow what her punishment will be, landing on the single thing in Kismet she can take away from Willow.

"You're not allowed to see Topher for one week," her mother says.

"Mom!" Willow pleads. "No! I mean—I get it. You're mad. But Topher's the only friend I have here. The only one I can talk to about the berries. Mom, I know . . ." She pauses. "I know about the magic. Mom, we need to talk about it."

"Oh, I know you know all about it," her mother snaps. "But don't change the subject. Tonight we will not be having that discussion. Tonight you will go to your room and stay there. I'm too angry to talk to you now."

Willow obeys, knowing she was wrong to just take off like that. On her way upstairs, she catches a glimpse of Wisp, who is safely curled up in front of the TV. He gives her a wave and a small smile of understanding.

Willow goes to their room, puts on her pajamas, and climbs into bed. Cora brings her a tray of food. But even though she was starving earlier, Willow is so tired now that she barely finishes half of it before falling asleep.

That night, she dreams of Wisp and her when they were little. They are running free through the woods, climbing high into the tree house their dad built for them and lying on their backs on the floor. The dream is so real Willow can actually feel Wisp's hand in hers, its warmth and its little-boy size. She lets herself drown in it.

She wakes late in the morning to tears on her cheeks. Will her dreams still be this vivid if something should happen to Wisp? Will she remember him this well after a month? In a year? Ten years from now?

She thinks of the berry and for a moment longs for its

assurance that this will not happen. But then she remembers that if she ate one, and Wisp dies, she will live it twice—the day of and the night before. The horror of that thought is enough to harden her resolve to pressure her mother to leave this town.

Willow makes her way downstairs, where her mom and Cora are standing drinking coffee. Her mother gives her a look and Cora hands her a plate—french toast and bacon.

Her mom tells Wisp to put on his coat. They are going to the hospital for a checkup. She tells Willow to stay put, even when Willow begs to go with them in the hopes of seeing Topher. But her mother's lips tighten, and so Willow closes hers fast. She thinks of the funniest Super Bowl ads she's ever seen and the best comedy routines she's ever heard, until her mom stalks out of the room to get her things from their bedroom.

"Did you see any blood-covered zombies or hairy, toothy werewolves out in the woods?" Wisp asks as he sits, swinging his feet, waiting for their mom to come back.

Willow can't help it. Today, his weird fascination with gory things makes her laugh.

Wisp looks up and grins, finally laughing with her.

After they leave, Willow's thoughts turn to Topher. She wonders what he is doing and if he is in as much trouble with his mom as she is with hers. Will they still have the party?

When he returned last night, did Topher give in and make his decision?

For all Willow knows, he ate one of the berries last night and made his commitment to the town, and all has been forgiven.

But for Topher's sake, she hopes he's still refusing.

Later that day, Cora tells Willow that Topher's party has been canceled—for now. She tells Willow this with lips tight and voice uncharacteristically low, and Willow can't help but feel badly for her part in squelching the celebration. But a part of her is relieved. This gives Topher more time to decide. Willow just wishes there was something she could do to help him.

That night, Willow finally corners her mom as they get ready for bed. She blocks the door so it will be impossible for her mom to avoid the conversation.

"Mom," Willow says, "we have to talk about those berries and what's going on in Kismet. We can't stay here. This place . . . the magic . . . it's not normal."

Her mom sighs and finally turns to face her. "Yes, it's odd, Willow, but don't you think in a way it would be strangely comforting to know your future?"

"No. I think it would be awful," Willow says, "always knowing what's going to happen to you before it does, every day. It would make life really boring."

Her mom gives her a look and shakes her head. "You think that now. But you might change your mind."

"I would never change my mind," Willow says. "I'm just glad I'm not Topher. I feel sorry for him, having to make that decision."

Her mother bites her lip but says nothing more.

In that moment, Willow realizes that her mom is unable or unwilling to see the problem with staying in Kismet and accepting the berries. If her mom doesn't snap out of it shortly, Willow might have to someday make the same decision Topher has to.

She needs to talk to Topher quickly. Together they have to find a way to beat the waters and these berries with their predetermined future. They both have a lot at stake—Topher, his imminent decision; Willow, her mom's scary indecision.

Willow might be forbidden to see Topher, but there are ways to run into him accidentally. She has to.

She goes to the diner for dinner with Mom and Wisp. But Topher is not there.

She goes with Wisp and Mom to the hospital. But he is not there either.

She would text him if she had a cell phone. But she doesn't, and he doesn't.

He never stops by Cora's to see her either, so Willow is left to wait and wonder.

Is Topher okay?

On Thursday, Mom and Wisp are at the hospital again. Cora is napping in the front room.

Willow gathers up her coat, stealthily slips out into the dazzling brightness of a sunny winter's day, and heads toward the lake to skate, hoping that Topher might be there.

But again, no sign of him. Willow sees only Grace, alone, skating on the far side.

Willow walks around the end of the lake and sits on the bench. She slips on the skates she used a week ago, stands up, and steps out onto the ice.

Soon Grace glides up beside her, having completed her neat little skating circle. "Nice of you to help Topher miss his party."

Her eyes are icier than the lake water frozen below Willow's feet.

"I didn't *help* him miss it," Willow protests. "We were only going for the morning. We should have been back in time for the party. How were we supposed to know about the storm? *We* didn't dream our day."

"Ever listen to weather reports?" Grace snaps.

"We didn't think—"

"No, you didn't!" Grace interrupts.

"You can have Topher's party some other time," Willow protests. "I don't see what the big deal is."

Grace rolls her eyes. "Topher hasn't made his decision yet.

But if he doesn't decide soon, the town will force him to do it. Not wanting to stay isn't like him. It's not like anyone here. What did you say to him?"

Willow shakes her head. She didn't say anything. It was Topher who told her the magic isn't what he wants. He's the reason she went from thinking it was amazing to seeing it for what it really is. But when she looks at Grace, she understands why the town has chosen to stay so isolated. Seeing people who still have a choice and have not committed to the town must be difficult once you've abandoned that option.

Grace snorts. "You act like you know everything, like you're better than us, so cool, coming into town all new and shiny-like. Like you're something different, something special. But you're not."

"What's that supposed to mean?" Willow snaps back. She isn't trying to be difficult. She didn't plan to have a car accident that would deliver her family here to make Topher's life tougher than it already is. The more she thinks about it, the more she realizes that the magic here is actually to blame.

Grace grins at her.

Suddenly, Willow doesn't want to know. She wants to stop Grace from talking. Willow wants to shut Grace up.

But Grace leans close, her dark eyes piercing into Willow's. "Do you want to know what your mom did with Cora a few nights ago?"

Willow feels a sudden quivering, like trees shivering in the wind with storm clouds on the horizon or a freight train coming down the tracks without brakes. She wants to press her hands to her ears. She wants to shout at the top of her lungs and drown out Grace's hateful, spiteful voice.

Willow stumbles backward, landing hard on the snowy ground. But Grace follows her, leaning down, close to Willow.

"Your mother has already agreed to the town terms. She's agreed to stay in Kismet. She ate a berry," Grace hisses. "So you are now a full-blown member of Kismet, just the same as the rest of us."

Willow wants to tell her she is wrong. Her mom would have talked to her about the decision before daring to agree to stay.

But then, her mom hasn't been worried at *all* lately. Is it because there is *nothing* for her to worry about anymore?

And Willow knows in that moment that Grace is telling her the truth.

Grace grins. "Welcome, Willow. Welcome to Kismet."

Then Grace laughs a little and skates away, leaving Willow sitting on the ground by the side of the lake, her heart oozing hurt and her spirits sinking, sinking toward the bottom of those magical waters of Kismet.

CHAPTER 26

S he sits in the snow, the seat of her jeans getting soaked, but Willow does not move. How could her mother have done this? How could she make this decision without discussing it with Willow?

Her mother has eaten the poison and accepted the town terms, and now her mother is stuck here for good. What will her dad say?

Willow's mind scrambles for a solution to this awful news she has just received. But she can think of no clock-turning, time-twisting way to undo this.

She is so deep in finding possible fixes that she does not notice anything around her until he sits down beside her in the snow, his breath frost-filling the air.

"Grace is wrong. You are special," he whispers. "At least to me."

Willow turns and sees him smile, but she can't even manage to answer him or to thank him for this kindness. She is still too brain-blown about her mother.

He nods across the lake. "Let's get hot chocolate. Let's talk."

She's cold. Her bottom is soaked. Her mind is numb. Things really can't get much worse. So she stands up and follows him toward the diner. He strides along the path around the lake while Willow trudges behind him, heavy-footed.

Inside the diner, Topher pulls a pair of sweatpants from his backpack and hands them to her. Willow looks at them and recoils.

"Did you eat a berry?" she asks.

"No," Topher says, looking at her puzzled. "Why would you think that?"

"Because you knew I needed these." She points to the sweatpants.

"I was going to go skating later, so I brought an extra pair," Topher says. "It was a coincidence. Not magic."

"Then how did you find me today?" Willow asks.

He turns red. "I was finally able to slip out. I got to Cora's and just saw you leave. I followed you and had almost caught up to you when I saw Grace."

She doesn't know whether to believe him. She doesn't know if she can trust anyone right now.

But Topher is right. She is cold. She is wet. And she is sad for her mother.

She goes to the bathroom and wiggles out of wet jeans and slides on dryness. Something stirs in her with the comfort of these warm clothes, and anger is soon filling the hole of her confusion and hurt.

She stomps her way back into the restaurant, where Topher has two cups of hot chocolate and a seat waiting for her.

"Did you know my mom ate a berry?" Willow asks. "Did you know she agreed to stay here?"

"I'm sorry, Willow. I did try to warn you," Topher says sadly. "The decision to join Kismet is not an easy one to make. I know that. You'll know too when you're thirteen."

And suddenly Willow is struck with the cold reality. She is trapped now too, bound tight like a fly caught in a spider's intricate web. Why did that not occur to her right away? It should have.

It is not just her mother who has agreed. If her mom has given her pledge to the town, then she has made the choice for Willow also. Her mom is not just a fate-knowing mother; they are now a future-knowing *family*. Willow will now *have* to make a choice when she is thirteen, just like Topher. The thing she feared has *already* come true.

Horror hits her hard in the gut. It is as if she is stuck in an elevator that will not move, or buried alive in a coffin, or tied inside a sack that is dropped into the sea.

Willow knows the truth—the whole truth. She gasps, and Topher nods. He has seen that the whole picture has come into focus for her.

"My-m dad . . . ," Willow stutters out.

"You can't tell him," Topher says. "The magic has to remain secret unless the town decides to invite him to join."

"What would they do to me if I *did* tell him?" Willow asks, sarcasm now a weapon of choice. "Make me stay here, huh? They can't force me."

Topher shakes his head. "No, they'll just deny it if you tell him. But that's if he can get here. If he can find his way in. Only the berries can decide that."

"Then I'll let him in," Willow says.

"You don't have a key," Topher reminds her. "But maybe you could convince him to come here too? To maybe stay? So you could all be together. You know, Willow, some people actually like knowing their fate. The colonel came here after being in a war. He is thankful for the certainty in every day after the hardness of battle. And Cora's husband abandoned her, which shocked her terribly. She says she wants to know ahead of time if she is going to have a tough day. Most people who live here grew up this way and are used to it, but there are others who have had sad things in their lives, and they appreciate being prepared for difficult times. Maybe your father would feel that way, with Wisp being sick?"

Willow thinks about this, but only for a minute. Her dad did not want to baby Wisp or change his diet or cushion him from hard things. She shakes her head.

"He won't, and I won't stay here either," she says, anger rising hot like steam as she tries to deny this awful situation she finds herself in, the same situation Topher is in. "I won't stay here. I won't. I want to do other things, see other things. I want to go to college. I want to dance under the stars by the sea and go skydiving and be a writer and live in New York City. I want to travel the world. Nobody can make me stay here!"

"That's true," Topher says softly. "They can't."

And he is right. They cannot.

If Willow wants her dreams to come true, in a little less than a year, she will have to leave her mom and Wisp and go back to her dad. But how can she just leave them?

"But there's free will," Willow says, her voice warrior fierce. "We have the freedom to make our own decisions. No one can deny us that."

"Of course there is, and you can choose," Topher reminds her. "But then there is fate, a future already determined for you. That's what the magic is—your fate or future revealed. And you cannot change fate."

Willow thinks on this.

Fate.

Fate or free will?

Are we free beings? Or does some unseen hand decide our lives?

If a child gets sick, is it for some reason? Or is it just random that Wisp's body should not be as strong as another's?

If Willow had been born a slave or a child who went hungry, would there be some rationale for that? Or is it just bad luck?

It is comforting to think there is a purpose to suffering— some why and wherefore that humans are not wise to. But that leaves everyone boxed in, soldiers following orders rather than butterflies taking wing.

Willow does not know what to do with these unanswerable doubts, these soul-searching questions. She does not know what to do for herself or for Topher. They are both stuck. Trapped—no matter what kind of worm wiggling Willow can think of. Trapped. She is nauseated at the thought of it all.

"You know you're not alone, Willow," Topher says. "I'm here."

But it's not like the other day when they went skating. His words can no longer make her heart hum.

Now she is brain troubled, soul sick. She needs to see her mom.

Willow stands up.

"Willow?" Topher says, his voice uncertain and whisper thin. "Tomorrow at nine they are going to make me choose. There'll be a meeting. I have to decide."

Willow can't even force out a word. She thinks of the Middle Ages and the reasons the plague spread so quickly and how they eventually found a way to stop the disease, but this time, thinking about other things she's learned or seen no longer calms her.

"I have to go," she manages to say, heading to the door.

Willow walks out, into the cold and away from the diner. She does not look back, but eventually, she hears Topher call, "Please be there tomorrow, Willow. I really want you there."

Willow wants to cry at his request. Topher was her hope, her bright-side savior, her shield against all sad things. Now she is just as trapped as he is.

Soon she is on the porch of Cora's house. The door opens, and her mom stands there, knowledge shining bright in her eyes.

"We need to talk," Willow tells her.

Her mom nods. "Yes. I know."

CHAPTER 27

When she finally gets upstairs and confronts her mother, Willow's anger roars out from her in a fireball of force. "How could you?"

"How could I not?" Mom asks. "For Wisp."

Wisp again. Always Wisp.

But guilt, for the first time, takes a backseat to this new imprisoned beast in Willow. She is a cornered animal with nowhere to go.

"But you decided for *me* too," Willow yells as she walks about the room. "Without asking me or talking to me about it."

"No," Mom says, holding up her hand as if to fend off the fury that is rippling in waves of heat from Willow's body. "I didn't choose for you. You will choose for yourself when the time comes."

"But what choice do I have?" Willow asks.

"Of course you have a choice, Willow," her mother says. "If you want to go back to Vermont and live with your dad, you can go. I'll let you do that, if that's what you really want."

"But I can't come back here then," Willow says. "That's it. You know the rules. Either you accept your future as the waters and berries determine it, or you are no longer welcome. If I leave, I may never see you or Wisp again."

"How can you reject this amazing magic?" Mom says, her tone calm and steady. "This magic can stop my uncertainty. I now have the chance to see ahead, to stop worrying for the day about Wisp when all along he was going to be fine. It's a chance we will never get again."

"You took that chance for you," Willow says. "Not for me or for Wisp, but for you."

Her mother nods. "Yes, for me. Do you know how comforting it is to know what is going to happen tomorrow? To wake in the morning and know how his day will unfold, to know he'll be fine all day, or at least have everyone prepared if he isn't going to feel well? Those berries are a miracle. I will always know what lies ahead for him *and* for me. And . . ." She smiles. "And I will know a whole day before he does, when he is completely cured. I can finally lay down this awful anxiety."

For a moment, Willow feels her mother's pain, and her relief in letting go of it. And Willow's heart pumps a sad swish of sympathy for her mother. But then she thinks of what their days will look like, always the same as what they saw the night before. She feels tears at the corners of her eyes.

She shoves the tears away, like a hammer striking iron. She cannot appear uncertain. Her mother must understand. Willow finally manages to find the courage to shout the words she knows her mother refuses to acknowledge. "Wisp may never be cured! He could die. I heard Dad say the doctors told him that."

There. She said it. Her mother's eyes harden.

"He will get better," her mom says, turning her face away. "Stop saying silly things like that."

"He may not!" Willow yells. "And if he doesn't, one day, when you eat that berry, Mom, you might see him die a whole day before he does. And then you'll have to watch it all over again. And I'll be gone, because I will not, *will not* stay here. And you will be stuck here alone without anyone."

"Wisp . . . ," Mom begins again.

But Willow is having none of it. "Wisp! Wisp!" she manages to spit out. "It is always about Wisp. You have destroyed everything in the hope of saving Wisp."

Willow hears a flurry of footsteps outside the bedroom door and her heart sinks.

Wisp has heard everything.

Her mom cries out for her to stop, but Willow ignores her. Instead, she runs after her brother, down the stairs and out the door. But Wisp moves quickly—faster than she has seen him move in a long time without their mom there to make him slow down. Willow is soon panting as she follows him out into the snow. He weaves from building to building, and Willow hurries after him, wondering how he is able to run this fast.

She finally catches up to him, sitting on the bench by the lake.

She stills her guilt-sick heart, slows her heavy breathing. She sits down beside her brother.

The sun is setting, and the town is quiet. Drawn home for dinner, the skaters have left the ice. The last rays of sunlight beam across the solid surface, dancing their way toward the end of the day. Night has not yet drawn the shades, and so the lights have not been thrown onto the darkening lake.

"I'm sorry," Willow says. "I didn't mean everything I said to Mom, and I didn't mean to keep a secret from you."

"I know," Wisp says, though there are tears in his eyes.

His little hand finds hers. He has forgotten his coat and mittens, and Willow has forgotten hers too. They are both cold, and Willow puts her arm about him, drawing him to her.

"So that's Topher's secret?" Wisp finally asks. "There's magic in Kismet?"

"How much did you hear?" Willow asks.

"Everything, I guess," Wisp says. "That by eating some kind of berry Mom will know what will happen the next day? And you can choose if you want to eat one of the berries or not? If you don't, you have to leave and not come back?"

Willow nods. She isn't sure how much she is allowed to reveal, and for a second, she fears what her punishment might be for telling him. But she can't help that he overheard. "That's the basics of it, I guess."

Wisp smiles, a slow smile that tickles his face.

"What?" Willow asks. "What's so funny?"

"I knew it," Wisp says softly into the evening, peacock proud of himself. "I knew there was something weird about this town. Remember the first night, when Cora put that bed and bucket in our room without even knowing about me yet? I knew it. I just knew it." He giggles. "I couldn't figure it out exactly, but I knew it was something. And now I know that I was right. I was right."

He is bouncing with happiness.

"Yes, now you know," Willow says slowly. She doesn't blame him. She was excited by the magic when she first discovered it too.

"You wish Mom would change her mind about staying, though?" Wisp asks. "Why?"

Willow sighs. "Knowing the future isn't as great as I thought it would be."

"Can you change what happens to you?" he asks as Willow sees him finally processing the magic of Kismet.

Willow nods, plowing on even though she is unsure whether she should or is even allowed to. But how can she leave her brother in the dark now? "Little things, but not the big ones. If you eat a berry and then try to change the way the day is arranged for you, your head hurts terribly. In Kismet, they don't believe you should change things that are meant to be. They believe everyone's future or fate is predetermined, and you can do nothing about it."

"So they like knowing what's coming?" Wisp asks.

Willow shrugs. "They say they do."

"Do you believe in fate?" Wisp asks.

Willow pauses. "I think we are all born with free will, Wisp, the ability to determine our own future. You shouldn't give up that choice. I think it's wrong to let some magical berries decide your day for you."

Wisp is quiet for a moment. "So everyone here has agreed to knowing what will happen before it does every single day?"

"Yes, after they turn thirteen," Willow tells him. "They eat a berry every night."

"Where do they get it?" Wisp asks.

Willow nods toward the brick building. "From a bush they grow there in a little room inside. The bush and its berries are fed from the waters of this lake, which have magical powers."

Wisp's eyes follow Willow's finger as she points. He stares at Kismet's town hall.

"So what are we going to do?" Wisp asks her.

"It's more like what is Mom going to do," Willow says.

Wisp turns to his sister and laughs. "You are so smart most of the time, but not always, Willow. You have a choice. That's what you believe. So what are *you* going to choose?"

Willow looks down at her brother. He's right. She does have a choice. And she doesn't *have* to wait until she's thirteen to make it.

CHAPTER 28

Willow lies in bed that night, unable to sleep. Her mind flits and flies. Her stomach rumbles and tumbles. But her head knows where her heart lies.

While predictability has its advantages, isn't it the surprises in life that make it sing? The rainbow after a storm? The tongue as it drinks after having been deprived of water on a long, dusty road? A kiss when two people have been parted for many days? Hard times as well as sweet times. They are the two sides of life, and Willow does not see how you can try to slide by the one, only savoring the other—and still have the ability to experience a truly lived life.

And so, in the darkest part of the night, when all of Kismet sleeps, Willow slips from her bed and goes to the kitchen. She picks up the receiver. In less time than there is to take back a word, she speaks out a plan.

When she hangs up the receiver, she stands there for a moment, hoping she has done the right thing. And then she heads back upstairs to tell Wisp what she has started.

The next day dawns with dazzling clarity. Sunshine sparkles on the snowy mounds that line the driveways and roadways of Kismet, Maine. It glints through snow-laden trees and glimmers on icy surfaces. Sadness seems an impossibility in the face of so much sunshine. And yet heartbreak may be on the horizon, for it is a day for decisions.

Willow closes her eyes against the glare. Her mind swims in circles, and her stomach flips with worry. Today will not be an easy day. She has no idea what Topher will do. She only knows what she has chosen.

She dresses slowly, reluctant to start the events that will unfold in an hour's time.

When she goes downstairs, her mother will not look at her. But even so, Willow can see that her mother's eyes are red-rimmed and swollen. Cora too is unusually quiet. They both know what the day holds, and Willow knows they already know what she has done.

And yet they will say nothing to alter the day. They will not try to convince Willow to change her mind. They will allow the day to progress the way the water and the berries have had them dream it. They believe it is their fate, their unchangeable future. And so they must follow the day as given and let it all play out, accepting what the berry has chosen, forfeiting their right to choose. It is what they, as members of Kismet, have agreed to. It is why they stay here.

Willow watches, and though she is sad, she is glad for her choice.

"I'll go on ahead," Cora says to Willow's mother. "Wisp should stay here."

Willow's mother nods.

Willow tries to eat some breakfast, but nothing wants to go down. Her brother pulls up a chair next to her. He lays his head on her shoulder.

"We need to go," her mother says a few minutes later, her words stiff as marching soldiers.

"Why can't Wisp come with us?" Willow asks. She wants to be with her brother as long as possible.

"Only twelve-year-olds and older can be at the Decision Ceremony," her mother tells her. "But after Topher makes his choice, all the children in town will join us either to celebrate or to see him go and say goodbye."

"You know what he's going to do, don't you? Can't you tell me?" Willow asks.

"I know what the berry showed me," her mother replies, frown lines deepening at the corners of her mouth. "But unlike the rest of us, Topher has not eaten one yet. He is not subject to their magic. Children's unpredictability is why they must commit when they are thirteen to try and keep things stable. It's slightly possible that Topher could change his mind at the last minute, so no, I won't tell you what I saw."

Her voice is firm, and so Willow says nothing more. She whispers goodbye to Wisp, holding him tight, until her mother clears her throat with impatience. Then Willow follows her mother out into the cold.

It is a somber group that makes their way to the town hall, the sound of everyone's boots crunching on the hard-packed, salted snow echoing eerily in the silent streets. Willow isn't sure whether everyone is grim because of Topher's decision or because of what Willow herself has done.

At the town hall, everyone gathers in the large room. The little door leading to the berry bush now stands open. The merry tinkle of the waters bubbling their way toward the lake fills the hall.

The room is still decorated, although the balloons droop, and some of the streamers have escaped their tape. Still, the fiddlers wait, hoping, Willow guesses, to strike up a happy tune should Topher agree to the town terms.

Cora is at the front of the room, a bowl of berries in her hand, their ripe gold color and blue and green stripes glowing with invitation. Beside Cora stands the colonel. When everyone is finally inside, the colonel steps forward.

"Welcome." His voice is strong, though his eyes seem moist, and Willow notices a trembling in his hand. Even the military man seems to be having a hard time, knowing what might come.

"Today, Topher Dawson must make a decision," the colonel continues. "As we all know, at age thirteen, or when you are invited to join . . ."

Here he pauses and looks at Willow's mother. His eyes swing

then toward Willow, and for a minute, Willow feels guilt rise in her gut. Then his eyes move on.

". . . you must make a decision," the colonel continues. "Do you want to be a part of Kismet or not? Topher Dawson is thirteen. He has been given a chance to see the benefits of knowing his future, of being prepared, of the certainty and direction the berries can give him. But in the end, it is his choice.

"Topher, please step forward and tell the town the choice you have made."

Topher walks slowly to the front. When he turns, his eyes meet Willow's. Then they swing away from her and toward his mother and his brother Joe Joe. He opens his mouth. Everyone leans forward. Will he stay or will he leave?

"I . . . ," he says, then stops. He looks down at the floor. "I can't," Topher finally says, his voice barely a whisper. "I'm sorry, Mom."

Everyone shudders with a loud collective gasp of distress. The band lays down their instruments. Dr. Dawson's shoulders begin to shake with quiet tears. Everyone was obviously still hoping.

Beside his mother, Joe Joe takes her hand, while Old Woman Wallace puts an arm around her waist to hold her up.

The colonel puts his hand on Topher's shoulder. "Then I'm afraid it's time to go, son. Annie will be on the other side of the bridge to take you out." He pushes Topher through the crowd and toward the front door. The townspeople follow. Willow's heart beats faster. Her own betrayal will soon be revealed.

As they walk through town toward the wall and the gate, the younger children join the group to say goodbye. Wisp is soon beside Willow and her mom. He takes Willow's hand and squeezes it tight as they walk.

They are a sea of people now, tidal-waving Topher away. There is no turning back for him. He will be pushed, pushed by the power of the berries and the beliefs of this town until he lands on shores unknown to him.

In front of her, Willow can see the rigid tightness of Topher's back, the methodical way he plants his feet as he heads toward the gate, the way his eyes never leave the ground. He is like a man condemned.

Then they are at the gate.

The colonel takes out his key and opens the portal. The gate swings easily in, and the crowd surges through. On they push in their journey toward the river and the road to the real world.

Ten minutes becomes twenty minutes. And then Willow hears it—the sound of turbulent waters, greedy and grasping, rushing and running in their quest to reach the lake.

As Willow approaches with the townspeople, there is a sudden rippling of something forming over the waters. The outline of a bridge begins to shimmer into focus.

Willow sucks in her breath. She says a prayer that what she tried to set in motion has worked.

At last, the bridge appears, solid and real, connecting Kismet with the outside, unaware world.

On the other bank, a truck and two cars idle. In front of the truck stands a woman, her face mottled with anger.

Near the cars stands Willow's dad. And beside him, another man waits, a man with dark hair and river-bottom-brown eyes.

"Dad!" Topher shouts in happy surprise.

CHAPTER 29

The townspeople all stop a few hundred yards from the bridge. Dr. Dawson grabs Topher's arm.

"Cora!" the woman on the other side of the lake shouts angrily, pointing at Willow's and Topher's fathers. "I thought I was to take Topher if he left? And who is this other man? Did you call these people? And if you did, why did you not tell me?"

Cora steps forward. "I'm afraid I did not call them, Annie." She turns and her eyes rest on Willow. The eyes of everyone swing toward Willow too.

Willow's stomach drops, but she gathers her courage like a general gathers troops. She takes a step forward.

"I called my dad," she says. "And I asked him to track down Mr. Dawson, in case Topher decided to leave. I thought it would be better for Topher to go with his father rather than having to live out there without any of his family at all."

Willow looks over at Topher, who mouths "Thank you" to her.

"That's not the way we handle things here in Kismet," the colonel reminds Willow. "To us, we are all family, not just Topher's dad."

"I know you feel that way, but that doesn't make it right," Willow says. "None of this is right."

"That isn't for *you* to decide!" Grace yells at her, her glare malicious as always.

"But it is," Willow argues. "The choice *is* mine to make. It's *yours* too. You *all* have a choice."

"You don't understand, honey," Layla calls to Willow. "We want to know what our future holds. We don't *want* surprises."

"That's not living," Willow points out.

"Says you!" Old Woman Wallace hollers.

"But it doesn't change anything," Willow continues, wishing they could see. "Even if you know pain is coming, you end up still suffering through it—twice. Once the night you dream it, and then again next day. The berries didn't stop you all from being sad that Topher is leaving or Dr. Dawson from shedding tears over it."

"But they prepare you," the colonel says, his lips tight. "You are ready for the pain."

Willow pauses with these words. He is right. For someone who has suffered in battle, knowing must be like salve to an unexpected wound. Willow gets this.

"Okay," she says slowly. "Yes, maybe you're prepared. But you are still giving up your right to choose how your day goes.

You are letting a berry and magic waters decide that for you. Don't you want to be in control of your own destiny? Why would you let a bush decide your life for you?"

"Because it hurts not knowing," Cora yells. "When someone leaves you or something terrible befalls you, the shock hurts. It's comforting to know what will happen before it does."

"Besides," Angeline says, "it's our fate. And you can't change fate, Willow. I told you that before."

Again, Willow recognizes some sense in what they say. Cora, having been hurt, wants no more of it. Can Willow blame her? And Angeline has grown up with this way of life. She knows no other.

And yet something inside Willow rebels and revolts. She cannot give up calmly and let this predetermined way of life win. And so she tries again.

"When you fall in love or have your first kiss, isn't the surprise of that awesome?" she asks. She sees Topher redden. He laughs a little, and she smiles at him. Topher, at least, understands, and this understanding lifts her spirits. "I mean, yeah, maybe you lessen the pain, but don't you also lessen your joy?" She thinks of the day spent sailing across the lake with Topher, the surprise of it. "Doesn't that bother you?"

She looks at her mom. "If you always know what's coming, how can you have the amazing pleasure that comes with the unexpected?"

Her mom says nothing.

The colonel steps forward. "That's enough, Willow. You can talk all you want, but this is the life we have chosen. The one we all want, including your mom. Now it's time for Topher to say goodbye. Be about it, son."

Topher closes his eyes for a minute, takes a deep breath, and then turns to his mom.

"I'm sorry, Mom," he says again, but this time his voice is shaking. "But I just can't."

His mother nods. Although she knew they would probably be here this morning with this decision, tears are still pouring down her face. "I understand. But I also hope, Topher, that you appreciate why I'm staying. They need me here. I grew up with them. I cannot abandon my town and my people."

Topher nods. "Of course I get it, Mom. Have you forgotten? I grew up here too."

She nods, and then he leans in and gives her a fierce hug. She hugs him back for a minute but then pushes him away. "Go," she says. "I'm glad your dad's here. I can rest easily knowing he's taking care of you."

Topher nods. Then he swings around and gives Joe Joe a hug. Finally, he leans down to pick up Taddie.

"I don't understand," Taddie cries when Topher whispers goodbye. "Why do you have to leave, Topher? Why can't Dad just come over the bridge? We could all stay here, couldn't we?"

Dr. Dawson takes Taddie from Topher's arms. "It's okay, Taddie. I promise you that I will explain all this to you in time. It's okay now. Topher is just going to live with Dad for a while."

"Time to go," the colonel says, coming to stand beside Topher.

Together, the colonel and Topher begin to walk away, heading toward the bridge. Topher's father moves closer to his side in order to meet them as the woman, Annie, begins carrying boxes of supplies across. As they near the edge of the bridge, Topher shrugs off the colonel's arm and runs toward his dad, who grabs him up in a bear of a hug. Their happiness in seeing each other rings right and true.

Willow takes a deep breath. Now she must make her decision. Her time has come.

Willow looks over at her mom. Her mom sighs, a sigh full of sadness and knowledge. She is well aware of what Willow is going to do, and Willow sees tears begin to stream down her mother's cheeks, just like Dr. Dawson's. And Willow wonders in that moment if her mother's broken heart might hold Willow in place, if she has the strength to see this decision through.

But then she looks at the townspeople, standing there, watching her, also held in place—but by a prison of their own making. They too know what she is going to do. But they will not even try to stop her. They do not have the courage to even try to battle the magic.

And in that moment, Willow is sure. She can't live like this. In her life, Willow will decide her own future all by herself.

She takes a step toward the bridge.

The townspeople wait. They know.

"Willow." Her mom's voice breaks on Willow's name, and Willow almost lets out a sob. How did Topher find the courage to do this?

Maybe if she tries one more time.

She turns and walks toward her mother. "Please," Willow whispers. "Come with me. We can be a real family again."

Her mom looks at her, and Willow feels her waver.

"Starr," Cora calls out. "Must we remind you that you've eaten a berry? If you try to change the future, you will suffer."

Willow's mom looks back at Cora, and slowly, she nods.

"I can't," she says to Willow. "I need to be here with Wisp, to know how he is."

"But if you stay, we'll never have a chance to be together as a family again," Willow says.

"I know, but by staying, I'm also giving Wisp a certain life," her mom reminds Willow. "A life where I can be the kind of mother I should be—fun, like I used to be before I began worrying every day. Wisp deserves that."

"And if he chooses to leave in a few years, when his time comes?" Willow asks.

Her mother sighs. "Then at least I will know that I have done what I needed to do as a mother."

Willow doesn't know what to say to this. There is nothing else she can think of to convince her mother.

"Willow," the colonel says, "if you're going to go, then you need to do it now."

The colonel's bossy tone irritates her. She reaches out defiantly, pulling on her mother's and Wisp's hands. She leads them both closer to the bridge, away from the townspeople.

Willow kneels down in the snow. She looks her brother in the eyes. "On the day you turn thirteen," she says, pointing to where their father waits for her on the other side, "I'll be there. Dad and I will both be there, waiting, on your birthday."

Wisp nods. "I know you will."

Her mom nods too, smiling a little.

There is nothing more to say. Willow stands. Her mother reaches out and brushes a lock of hair from her face. Willow bites back a sob, and her mother quickly wraps her arms around her. Willow holds her mother tight, breathing in her mother's scent for what might be the last time.

"Willow. Now," the colonel calls to them.

Willow bites back a snappy retort. After all, he is right. She has to leave sometime. So she forces herself to break away from her mother and turns to her brother.

"I'll miss you," she says. She hugs him close.

He whispers, "I'll work on Mom. Somehow I'll get her home. I promise. It'll be okay, Willow."

"How?" Willow asks.

Wisp smiles. "I'll figure it out. Go. Dad needs someone too."

He steps back—the little boy all man now.

"Go," he commands her. "Go with Dad."

Willow bites her lips. Tears tickle the corners of her eyes, but Wisp is firm. Finally, Willow nods her agreement.

She turns and begins to walk quickly onto the bridge, wanting to reach her father and Topher and his dad before she can change her mind.

But halfway across the bridge that separates Kismet from the rest of the world, Willow turns for one last look.

Her mother's eyes are swollen with sorrow.

"I love you, Mom," Willow calls back to her mother, "but you know, living like this means you've let fear win. So you see, you're just like Dad, who couldn't face the hard stuff either."

Then Willow turns again and begins to walk across the last half of the bridge. But she has only taken a few steps when she hears a voice.

"Willow! Wait!"

CHAPTER 30

Willow turns.

"You're right," her mother calls to her.

Willow pauses. Has she heard her mother correctly?

But already her mother is grabbing Wisp's hand and running toward the bridge, pulling him with her.

Willow's heart begins to gallop. They are coming! Her mother and Wisp are coming!

"Stop!" the colonel yells into the surprised silence suddenly surrounding them all. "Stop, Starr DuChard! This isn't to happen. You are not to go!"

But her mother keeps running.

It doesn't take long for the townspeople to overcome their shock at this change in their predicted future.

"Stop her! Get her!" come the cries.

James and the colonel run after Willow's mom and Wisp. Having brought her to Kismet and fed her a berry, they are not about to let her go.

Willow watches, stock-still, barely able to breathe as they

chase them. Her heart pumps in sickening beats and bursts. Will they make it?

Her mother is slower than her brother. If she does not pick up speed, James will have her in hand soon. Her mother must realize this too.

She lets go of Wisp, pushing him ahead of her. "Go!" she yells at him.

Wisp does not need to be told twice. He runs, his little arms pumping, his little legs churning. Soon he is at Willow's side. She grabs him, turns, and pushes him back toward their father.

"Go!" she yells to her brother. Then she turns back toward her mom.

Her mother is on the bridge, and Willow is almost certain she will make it, when suddenly, her mom lets out a piercing screech and drops to the ground, grabbing her head.

"Mom!" Willow yells, panic swelling her insides.

Her mother tries to lift herself up, to find purchase enough to stand. But she can't seem to manage it. Instead, she lets out another shriek and rolls into a ball, her arms pressed to her head as if a great weight is crushing her skull.

"It's the magic!" Topher cries behind Willow.

Willow's mom tries again. She pushes herself to her knees, crawls a few feet more, and then lets out a third and final painful cry before slumping over.

James and the colonel have reached the bridge now. But just as they go to step onto it, they too are forced to their knees. The magic trying hard to force everyone back to their predicted fate.

Willow's mom seems to have given up. She is no longer rising. Willow begins to run to her, when the bridge starts to shake beneath her feet.

"Willow!" Topher yells. "The bridge is collapsing!"

She doesn't want to stop, but panic rises in her. Has her moving made the structure less sturdy? Their car drove onto this bridge. How is it possible that Willow can have this strong an impact just by taking a step?

But she can't leave her mother there on a bridge that is falling to pieces.

Then her mother uncurls from her ball. She struggles to rise once more. She inches forward and then tumbles again. The bridge groans and shakes.

Willow's heart pounds as she weighs her choices.

"You have to get her!" Topher yells to her again.

Willow knows he's right. If she doesn't rescue her mother, she could end up where they almost were thrown that first night they came to Kismet—in the rushing magical waters below.

"Stay away, Willow!" the colonel shouts to her, holding his head, grimacing in pain. "Your mother is not meant to go with you. The magic has made that clear to us all and to her. You are to leave. She must not."

Her mom raises her head wearily. "Go on, Willow," she calls into the rising wind. "Take Wisp. Get out of here. I'm going back. I can't fight this pain, and I *did* make the choice."

Her mom pushes herself to her feet, turns, and begins to

head back toward the waiting townspeople, who even now are nodding with satisfaction at this decision.

But Willow cannot obey her mother—not this time. This time she will not just do as she is told. This time she will fight. She will be the gladiator her mother has always been for them. Willow will not let these townspeople and their magic berries decide her mother's fate. Their family future is for their *family* to decide!

At last, she makes herself move, to run to her mom, and with that choice, her feet seem to fly. She knows she is in a race against Kismet, for the colonel and James are already waiting, waiting to snatch her mother as soon as she nears the end of the bridge.

Willow pushes harder. She is close, so close.

She reaches out and grabs her mother's arm, yanking her away from the end of the bridge, and begins to pull her back toward the other side. Her mother lets out another scream of pain and drops to her knees again, but Willow continues pulling her toward her father and her brother, toward a life unknown.

"Stop!" the colonel demands. "Bring her back, Willow! Can't you see you're hurting her?"

But Willow will not listen. She will not stop. She will never stop trying to reunite her family, to live their life the way *they* decide.

She drags her mother after her, pulling and tugging. Her mother's body is limp from the pain, and her heaviness weighs on Willow.

"I can't. I can't help you," her mother cries. "I'm trying, but the pain is so bad."

"You can, Mom," Willow says. "We can do this. You've always been our fighter. But today, we're going to fight this together."

A rumble of thunder reverberates in the distance. The bridge gives a shudder. A flash of lightning splits the world around them in two. Thunder rolls down from the mountain like a monster about to eat its fill.

"We won't make it," her mother says, her teeth clenched from the pain in her head.

"We will," Willow says. "You're not alone. I'm here, and together, we can do this, Mom. Fight, Mom. Fight to be with us."

Her mother tries to stand again, struggling with everything she has against the pain that is the result of rebelling against the magic, this town, her fate.

A crack sounds behind them.

"Willow, hurry!" Topher calls. "The waters are destroying the bridge."

Willow swallows hard and pulls again on her mom's arms.

Then, suddenly, there is someone else there.

Willow looks up. Her father has come for them. He has come out onto the bridge. He has come to save her and her mother. At last, her father has found the strength to help them.

Together Willow and her father lift her mom, draping her arms across their shoulders. They drag her toward the other side as the bridge slowly collapses behind them. The sound the structure makes as it disintegrates is like the sound of an avalanche.

They run, bumping along with Willow's mom between them. And when they finally, finally, reach the other side, the bridge, at long last, gives way completely, the whole thing magically disappearing in the end without a single sound.

They stand on either side of the divide, staring at one another: a townspeople united, a family reunited.

They each have their beliefs, and who is to say which is right?

"You had better keep your mouth shut about what you've seen," Annie warns them before heading to her truck. "I'm out here, so I'll be keeping an eye on you. Don't you forget it."

"We won't say a word," Willow's mom manages to choke out.

Willow looks over at the other bank, with no way to reach it now, and nods her agreement. The secret of the magic in Kismet is safe, and really, who would believe her anyway?

Across the gorge of the river, Willow watches the colonel and Cora, Layla and James, Old Woman Wallace and Angelina and Grace turn away from them. Slowly, they and the others make their way back up the mountain toward a stone wall that lies hidden from most humans, to a locked gate that keeps the town contained in their certain and safe world.

Only Dr. Dawson remains for a minute more. She raises her hand to her lips and sends a kiss to Topher. He sends her one back, tears in his eyes. Then his father comes and puts his arm around Topher's shoulder.

"Come along, son. Let's go."

Topher looks at Willow. "Will I see you again?" he asks.

Willow smiles. "Of course. Who else could I talk to about what happened? I'll need to see you just to be sure I didn't dream it all."

Topher laughs. Then he turns to his father. "Okay, let's go home, Dad."

Home.

Willow watches Topher walk toward the car that will take him to his, and then she turns toward what she hopes is still her car.

Her father is holding her mother, whose color seems to be returning now that she is firmly on this side of her decision. Her parents cling to each other like storm-tossed survivors, which is what they are.

Willow watches as Wisp squeezes himself between them. He gives her a thumbs-up.

Willow would like to smile too, but she still isn't sure if her parents will *ever* knit themselves back together again completely. Yet in leaving Kismet, they have all decided that they are willing to accept that uncertainty.

The future lies before the DuChard family now—undetermined, unpredictable, a blur of possibilities, a potential pit of dangers, probably some sorrows, definitely some joys.

And Willow knows then, with the confidence that only someone who has seen her future *can* know, that the true magic of life lies in those days that are not yet known.

ACKNOWLEDGMENTS

Stories start with a seed of an idea, send out roots in a writer's mind, and finally blossom when pen is put to paper. But all manuscripts, like young plants, need dedicated gardeners to help them grow. I have had some wonderful ones during this book's maturation.

First and foremost, many thanks go to my agent, Liza Voges, for planting this story in fertile ground—I am so glad that we re-connected after so many years. And discovering that Eden Street Literary was based on a street in Bar Harbor was like finding a rose in mid-December. I consider you not only an agent extraordinaire and a fellow Mount Desert groupie, but a good friend, too.

To my editor, Kelsey Horton, whose enthusiasm shines through even in her emails, thanks for the thoughtful snipping and deadheading that left this manuscript leaner and finer than when it first was sown. We did some deep digs on this one, but your tender loving care and fruitful ideas have made this work so much stronger. Thanks for taking this writer on and letting my work out to enjoy the dawn.

To Pascal Campion, thank you for designing the most awesome book cover ever! You cultivated a magical rendering that perfectly captured the story in one simple snapshot. I love it!

To my copy editor, Colleen Fellingham, your careful nurturing of my work rid it of careless errors, numerous bugs, and other various detritus that could have killed it rather than letting it thrive. I thank you for all your patient pruning.

To the sales force at Delacorte . . . thank you for taking this painstakingly tended story and finally releasing it to (hopefully) be enjoyed by many. I so appreciate your help in ensuring that it continues to bloom and flourish in the months to come.

And to the newest addition in my own little garden of love, my soon-to-be son-in-law, John Tassinari. You have sunlit your way into our lives, and we are so happy to welcome you into our family. You are a true gentleman, a kind soul, a compassionate, caring man, and someone who I know will bring great joy to our daughter. And I know she loves you deeply, too. I truly could not be happier.

And finally, to the little threesome of people who, for so many years, have filled my life with true magic—Chris, Tobey, and Liza Duble. You three have been there for me through many a water-drenched day and dry desert moment. But more important, you have also been the ones who have showered me with hours and hours of incomparable love.

Together, you three, and now John, are the best bouquet of joy any woman could hope for! I love you four forever and always!

ABOUT THE AUTHOR

Kathleen Benner Duble is a critically acclaimed and award-winning author of many novels for children. Her books include *Phantoms in the Snow, The Sacrifice,* and *Quest.* She lives in Massachusetts when she is not adventuring in Maine or traveling the world with her husband and two daughters. For her, being a writer is a truly magical life. Visit her at kathleenduble.com and @KathleenDuble on Twitter.